MURDER ON THE MARSH

A gripping crime thriller full of twists

ANNE PENKETH

JOFFE BOOKS

First published 2016 by Joffe Books, London.

www.joffebooks.com

This book is a work of fiction. Names, characters, businesses, organizations, places and events are either the product of the author's imagination or are used fictitiously. Any resemblance to actual persons, living or dead, events or locales is entirely coincidental. The spelling is British English.

978-1-911021-83-4

For Betty

Chapter 1

Flesh and nail. Or was it nails only?

Sam Clayton had been playing classical guitar for so long that he couldn't really explain how his fingers obtained that sound from a string. He didn't usually think about technique. But today, nothing was going smoothly. With head slightly bowed, he was practising a tremolo which refused to flow evenly from his fingertips. He'd hoped his music in the stillness of his living room would clear his head. The students in the house next door were silent for once. Most weekends the wall was practically bouncing with the sound of heavy metal.

"Come on," he said out loud. Maybe it was just the wrong day to pick the *Recuerdos de la Alhambra*. He set down the guitar and picked up another score from a pile on the carpet. Flicking through it, he didn't even recognise his own pencil markings. His mind kept returning to the churchyard.

They'd been on the national news after the discovery of a shallow grave just inside the stone wall of the village church, three days after Jimmy Spratley was reported missing on the local marshes. The boy was only eight years old, and the little body had been mutilated, his heart torn out.

In the couple of years he'd worked for Anglian Constabulary, the most serious incident reported in the North Norfolk villages had been the theft of an outboard motor. Now there was a child killer on the loose, in Glaveny of all places.

The images of the open jacket, the ripped T-shirt and the hole gouged out where that small heart had throbbed, had haunted Clayton's dreams ever since. The officers who watched them dig up the body, though used to the sight of mangled car crash victims, had returned to their cars and vomited onto the tarmac. Some had needed counselling.

Clayton had informed the parents himself, taking with him a detective sergeant with a background in child protection. The family liaison officer was already at the house and let them in, her eyes flashing a warning.

The father stood behind her. "Couldn't you have done something to save our Jimmy?" He had jabbed his finger at them, his wife, silent on the sofa beside him, twisting and twisting her hands. In a flamingo pink mini-skirt and matching drop earrings she wasn't dressed for tragedy. Families never were.

"We did everything we could. The whole village came out to join the search, you know that, Mr Spratley," said Clayton.

He knew he sounded defensive, but what more could he tell them? In the milky pall of the mist, they'd combed every footpath, scoured every muddy channel, searched every bird hide as far as the Pelham windmill and beyond, startling the tourists out for the half-term holiday with their children. They'd taken out boats from Branstable Quay to the seal colony on Glaveny Point, peering through binoculars at the dappled shapes on the shingle, their almost human moans clinging to the breeze.

When the mist cleared, they'd sent people with sticks through the reed beds, back into the village and along alleyways lined with empty flint cottages, where they peered through the windows. They'd searched abandoned boats washed up by surge tides on the marsh and the old Lifeboat House used by the nature reserve wardens.

The vicar had rung the police after spotting a fresh mound of soil loosely covered by turf in the graveyard. He'd ranted on about "an illegal burial" on hallowed ground.

The boy's father had yelled at them. "But what does it mean? What are we supposed to do now? He was our only child!" A row of family photographs stood on the window ledge. One was a group shot of a child with seaweed for hair, being hugged by his parents.

"We're following up leads, Mr Spratley, we've got the whole force on the case. That's why we were called in," Clayton had said. Anglian Constabulary, based outside Norwich, handled all serious crimes in the outlying areas. He reached up to straighten his tie, his neck felt constricted. If only we had something to go on, he thought, watching a vein pulsating on Spratley's forehead.

"What kind of sicko would do a thing like that?" Spratley reached for his wife who crumpled, shuddering with sobs, against his shoulder. Her eyes were closed tight as though she was trying to shut out the horror.

The two detectives had left a few minutes later, seeing themselves to the door.

"I want you to get that bastard!" Spratley had called out as they made their way out. Clayton gestured to the liaison officer to stay behind with the bereaved couple.

As they drove off, the first TV crew was heading to the bungalow. Bloody journalists, thought Clayton. HQ wouldn't even have had time to appeal for privacy.

Spratley's question had resonated with Clayton ever since. What sort of monster would abduct a young boy, carve out his heart and then bury him where he was certain to be found?

So far forensics hadn't come up with DNA clues and they hadn't found the murder weapon as yet. It had to be some kind of hunting knife.

The villagers they'd interviewed had been no help. See no evil, hear no evil, speak no evil. Keeping to themselves, even after one of their own children had been murdered.

Clayton shook his head and kicked aside his footstool. Jimmy Spratley probably knew his killer, he thought. We'll have to go back and knock on more doors. But not today. It was his first day off in almost two weeks. He sighed and picked up his mug of cold coffee from the carpet. He took it into the kitchen and dropped it on the counter where it clinked against two other coffee-stained mugs.

What was the significance of the heart? They could only speculate. A satanic ritual? Some kind of perverted message from the killer?

The remains of Jimmy's heart had been discovered by a birder who'd heard the news about the murder. He'd noticed a clatter of seagulls circling over the marsh near the car park at Glaveny Point. He'd described to police how he'd looked through his binoculars at shreds torn from a chunk of blackened muscle the size of a fist. An animal, probably a dog judging from the teeth-marks, must have retrieved it from under a clump of samphire. Forensics had brought the whole lot back to the lab like a trophy. It didn't take them long to establish a match with Jimmy.

Clayton stepped over his guitar and tugged open a curtain by the French windows. The grass in the back garden glistened with fresh rain and his rusting lawnmower stood among weeds by the fence. He heard the muffled sound of his phone, which he traced to a pile of newspapers. He scattered them over the carpet with one hand.

It was the office. "What's up, Blake?"

"It's another missing person in Glaveny. A waitress from the Point Hotel."

Chapter 2

Clayton pressed the phone hard against his ear and shut his eyes. "What've we got?"

"Woman called Emma Dawson. She's not been seen since yesterday afternoon. She worked the lunchtime shift but didn't go back in the evening."

"Shit."

"The mist has come in again in Glaveny."

In North Norfolk the mist didn't descend from the sky, it rolled in from the sea, smothering the shingle and sliding across the marshland, its tongue licking the watery channels. Sometimes it could become blindingly thick in minutes, taking walkers by surprise. It often vanished just as quickly.

"Who told us?"

"Next door neighbour. Emma Dawson leaves her little boy with her. He's friendly with the Berrys' son. But she never showed up to collect him. The neighbour, Becky Berry, called us this morning."

Clayton looked at his watch.

"Where's the lad now?"

"Still next door. They're just off the main road."

"This is too much of a coincidence. I'm coming in. Make sure we've got as many uniforms out there as possible."

So much for his Sunday off.

He belched, picked up his half-eaten microwaved lasagne from the coffee table and stowed the guitar in its case. He dumped the food carton in the kitchen rubbish bin, pitching the fork into the sink where it disappeared into grease-stained water. His T-shirt felt taut over his belly. Ever since Claire had left, which was over a year ago now, he'd struggled to keep his weight down. Work kept getting in the way, just like it had got in the way of their marriage. Despite his resolve to run off the excess weight, his paunch was as solid as ever.

As he went upstairs to change, he heard pounding through the wall. The students must be there after all. He brushed his teeth, combed the fluff of his receding hair and ran downstairs.

He strapped himself into the VW and searched the glovebox for a CD. He debated whether to ring Julie Everett, the detective sergeant who'd accompanied him to see the Spratleys. She would probably hold it against him if he didn't call, even on her day off. She was chippy. She'll get over it, he thought, and rang DS Neil Pringle. Sometimes he just felt more comfortable with a male colleague.

* * *

An hour later, they stood outside a flint terraced cottage on a cul-de-sac that backed onto the Glaveny marsh. The mist had begun to recede, revealing a red-tinged carpet of samphire. A steady, fine drizzle dampened their macs. A family from the house opposite piled into a Range Rover and drove towards the main road.

A woman opened the cottage door, pulling her loose jumper down over her jeans. She looked to be in her early thirties.

"Ms Berry? Detective Inspector Clayton and Detective Sergeant Pringle, Anglian Constabulary," Clayton said. He always felt self-conscious reciting the name. It had been foisted on them following the merger of the Norfolk and Suffolk forces which had put an end to any pretence of friendly cooperation.

"You from Norwich?" She said it to rhyme with porridge in the local way.

Clayton nodded.

"Come in out of the rain." She spoke slowly and her eyes were glassy.

"Sorry, it's a bit of a mess." In the small room plastic toys formed a network of obstacles across a threadbare carpet. "The boys are upstairs."

"So Eddie's still with you?"

"That's right. He came round yesterday afternoon and has been here with my Jack ever since."

"Can we see him?"

"I guess. He's been crying. He's not his usual self at all. In fact he's not said anything since I called the police. Not a word."

Clayton wondered whether he should have called Julie after all. She did have a way with kids. They responded to her touchy-feeliness.

"He's usually as chatty as anything. Talks to himself all the time."

"And what made you worried about Emma Dawson?"

Becky Berry told him she took care of Eddie in return for the waitress taking her son to school every morning.

"On weekends as well?" Neil said. He looked up from his notebook.

Neil on a new case was like a Labrador puppy. He looked ready to roll on the carpet with his legs in the air every time they had a lead. A missing person so soon after a murder in the same village had him almost barking.

"Of course. She has to work weekends. But she's devoted to him. It's the first time she's not picked him up on time, even when she goes to the pub after."

"So why did you wait until today before calling the police?" said Clayton.

Becky was leaning heavily against the kitchen counter. "I called the hotel manager last night to find out where she was, but he said she hadn't turned up. He sounded more annoyed than worried. I thought there must be an explanation, and that she'd show up. Eddie bedded down with us last night but when there was still no sign of her this morning, we got really worried."

"Is Ms Dawson a reliable person?"

"Very. I'd trust her with my life. They love her at the hotel. She gets lots of tips."

"What about visitors? Boyfriends?"

"Emma came back to Glaveny after breaking up with her husband. She doesn't talk much about boyfriends and the like, she's quite private," she said. "I sometimes see the husband come to pick up Eddie." She paused. "But yes, there's been this Frenchman skulking around for the past few days."

A Frenchman? Skulking? Clayton stopped his note-taking. "How do you know he's French?"

"I saw him myself. I was behind him in the queue at the bakery. There's no mistaking that accent." She straightened herself against the counter. "A bit of exotica you might say. Makes a change in Glaveny."

"Who is he? A customer from the hotel?"

"I don't think so. Well, I don't actually know, but Eddie might."

"Can we see him? It won't take long."

Becky went upstairs slowly, holding tight to the banister and swaying slightly. She came down leading Eddie by the hand. He was a slight child with big eyes. His small face was puffy, the cheeks reddened and streaked with tears.

"Hello, Eddie. We're going to find your mummy, don't you worry about that," said Clayton, patting him on the shoulder. Eddie gripped Becky's hand, his dark cartoonish eyes staring up at Clayton.

"Did you see her with anyone yesterday?"

The boy looked up at Becky as though for approval. Becky squeezed his hand. "You can tell them. They're here to help."

The boy screwed up his face, then turned away from them, clinging to the folds of Becky's jumper, his fists clenched. Clayton and Neil looked at each other.

"It's alright, Eddie," said Clayton. "Can you just remember what time it was when you last saw your mum?"

The boy squirmed but still said nothing. He put his thumb in his mouth and sucked in his cheeks.

"Just try to remember," Clayton said gently. He definitely should have brought Julie. There were strict rules about interviewing children. "We know how much you love your mum. Were you out with her yesterday? Maybe walking on the marsh?"

"How about Friday?" Neil said. "Did you go out trick or treating?"

Becky answered. "Yes, they did, but they only went down our street. Eddie had a flashing light sabre and a cloak. It was great, wasn't it? They were both tucked up in bed by nine."

"Where? Here?" Neil said.

"No, Eddie went home, didn't you? His mum's off on Fridays." She stroked the boy's untidy curls. "There, there, never mind. Do you want to go back up with Jack?"

He didn't need asking twice. He picked up a red-and-yellow lorry from the floor, wedged it under his arm and ran upstairs.

Clayton turned to Becky. "You say Ms Dawson came back to Glaveny?"

"Yes, she was brought up here. But there's not much work, so when she left school she got a job waitressing in Norwich after her parents moved there."

"You got a key to next door?"

"Sure." She opened a kitchen drawer and handed him two keys with labels marked *Emma.* "You have to fiddle with it a bit in the lock then push hard to open the door. The other one's the back door."

"And did Emma go out much on the marsh?" Clayton asked.

"Oh yes. We all do. We love it. Before poor Jimmy died we let the kids go there all the time."

Neil was flicking through his notes. "What about the neighbours opposite?"

"City folk. London, I think," she said.

"And are you married, Ms Berry?"

"Yes."

"Your husband's not here though."

"No, he's a fisherman. Comes and goes with the tide." She gave a thin smile, and closed the door behind them.

* * *

They walked towards Emma Dawson's cottage next door. "What do you think, Sam?" Neil asked him.

"I don't like the sound of it." Emma Dawson had been missing for twenty-four hours already. Clayton thought of Jimmy Spratley, the last person reported missing in that village.

"That kid's traumatised," Neil said. "What if he knows something? And what's she on?" he added, with a nod in the direction of Becky Berry's.

But Clayton was bending down to examine the cottage's low sash windows, their paint peeling from the salt air. On the windowsill was a small violet in a pot, and a pumpkin looked out at them with a toothless grin. Above the front door, a sign announced that the cottage belonged to the village housing society.

"Let's just have a quick look round," said Clayton, pushing open the front door. It opened into a small living room separated from the kitchen by a counter. A mirror image of the Berrys'.

Switching on the light, they could see a box of toys on the carpet, and a television in the corner next to a stack of plastic chairs. The shabby covers of two armchairs were scarred with cat scratches. A low round table sat in the middle of the room. Clayton bent down to study a photograph of Eddie on his mother's knee, both of them looking straight into the camera. The boy was giggling. Was she tickling him? He didn't seem anything like the withdrawn child he'd just met.

He noticed two mugs on the counter beside a kettle, ready to be poured.

A couple of crayoned drawings were pinned to the wall. The first, of a blue sky, yellow sun and spiky green marsh grasses with two stick figures in the foreground, was signed in capital letters, EDY. The second, a picture of a brontosaurus in a swamp, must have been done more recently. Eddie's name was spelled correctly, and was surrounded by gold stars.

They went into the kitchen, trying not to touch or disturb anything. There were two small bowls on the floor, licked clean of their contents.

"Is it me or is it cold in here?" said Clayton, stepping back into the living room. He felt a clammy draught swirling around him. It seemed to pass from the room up the stairs.

"It's probably just the damp," Neil said. "We're right by the marsh, remember."

"I'm going up."

"Shall I look outside?" Neil held out his hand for the back door key.

Clayton went up the stairs two at a time. One room, with curtains open, was the child's bedroom, decorated with more pictures. Clayton could hear a faint scratching noise coming from inside the other upstairs room. He threw open the door and stepped back. "Jesus Christ!"

The cat must have been shut in the bedroom since the previous day. A furry black shape streaked past him, down the stairs and out of the front door.

Clayton found the light switch and peered inside the bedroom. The air felt as moist as his mildew-coated shower.

He jumped. A skull stared straight at him through baleful eye sockets.

Neil came up beside him. "Why would anyone keep a skull in their bedroom? This place is starting to give me the creeps."

Clayton inspected the object, which sat on top of a chest of drawers. It was carved from wood and hollow inside. He could see the grease of a nightlight at the base, and imagined it flickering in the dark, throwing shadows.

He heard a creaking noise coming from downstairs.

"Did you shut the back door?"

"I thought so. I'll go down again and check." Neil's boots echoed on the wooden stairs. Clayton took a last look round the bedroom, where condensation had formed on the window. Downstairs, he found Neil locking the back door.

"I could have sworn I closed it behind me," he said.

"What about outside? Anything there?" Clayton asked.

"An old pushchair in the yard. There's a shed but I couldn't see through the window. We'll have to come back."

A tap dripped over the kitchen sink. Neil turned it off.

Clayton tugged the front door closed behind them, and looked down the street. The cat was sitting on Becky Berry's window ledge, licking its fur with a pink tongue. It watched them through yellow slits as they went back to their car.

Neil opened his phone to call the office, but it was Clayton's that rang. He listened in silence, his eyes fixed straight ahead.

"Okay, we'll be right over. Get me forensics." He turned to Neil. "They've found a body in a boat at Branstable."

Chapter 3

They had a meeting with the DCI in ten minutes. Meanwhile, Clayton was in the office giving the wastepaper basket a good kicking. Screwed up balls of paper jumped about like fireworks. He heard a sound and looked round. Julie was standing by his desk with arms folded and an accusing look on her face.

"Thanks for the phone call yesterday."

"Don't you start. I thought you deserved a day off."

She held her ground. Her blonde hair was tied in a bun as tight as her features. "Just so long as you know who's supposed to be the child specialist round here."

"Come off it, Julie. How were we to know that we'd end up interviewing the son of a dead waitress? You weren't down to work anyway."

She watched in silence while he collected the discarded papers and dropped them back in the bin.

"Come on, let's pick up Neil and get this over with," he said, grabbing his notebook.

Detective Chief Inspector Charlotte Bligh always looked as if she had a stomach ache. She was sitting on her desk with her feet swinging, waiting for them.

She gestured to the chairs, slightly below her level. "Congratulations on making Anglian Constabulary a national laughing stock."

Neil stroked a large plaster at the base of his thumb. Julie looked at the floor.

"First we have a dead boy, attracting nationwide media coverage, and now a young woman found strangled to death in the same village. Don't you think this is starting to look a little bit out of control?"

Clayton opened his mouth to speak, but she cut him off, tapping her pen on the desk. "What are the leads? First of all, the boy. Do we know whether he was tampered with?"

"Forensics said there was nothing to indicate sexual assault, no, ma'am."

"That's a relief. A child abuse case would be radioactive in Norfolk."

"We've gone through the sex offenders register, of course."

"And?"

Clayton turned to Neil.

"Just one in the neighbourhood. In his seventies. And he's got dementia."

"Most murderers are known to their victims. Let's not forget that. What did they say at the school?"

"The headmistress at Jimmy Spratley's school has gone through the CVs of all her staff, just to be on the safe side," Julie said.

"So as things stand, we've pretty well ruled out sexual motivation, ma'am," said Clayton.

Bligh paused, looking down at her shoes. "What about the woman?"

Clayton opened his notebook. "We've not got all the tests back yet. Here's what we know so far. A dog walker at Branstable Quay noticed strands of hair peeking out from under the tarpaulin of a small boat hauled onto the bank of the creek, while his dog was peeing against it.

When he got closer, he saw smudges of what looked like blood on the side. He called us after seeing a shape under the tarpaulin. We found Emma Dawson's body in the boat, her clothes drenched in blood. Strangled with barbed wire."

"And the boat owner?"

"A guy from London. Not used the boat since the summer."

"Do we think the two killings are linked?"

"We don't know yet, ma'am. The only link is that they both occurred in the same village."

"So what do we have so far?"

Clayton leaned forward in his chair. "We've got footprints. Boot prints in the mud where the body was heaved into the boat."

"What size?"

"Nines."

The DCI nodded. "Tyre treads?"

"Not by the boat, no. The car park is right there though."

"And that's useful — or not?"

"No. Not with all the comings and goings."

Bligh sighed. "That's what I thought."

Clayton hesitated. "She's got a tattoo on her ankle."

"A tattoo? What sort of tattoo?"

"A daisy. Well, a flower anyway. Looks like a daisy to me."

Bligh laughed. "Doesn't everyone under forty have a tattoo these days?"

"Of course. But we don't know the significance of it yet."

"It seems that you haven't figured out the significance of very much at all. What about the woman's child? Any clues there?"

"He's been struck dumb. He's not said anything since his mother disappeared. But the next door neighbour said she'd been seen around with a Frenchman."

Bligh raised an eyebrow. "Okay. Get me an update on the French connection as soon as possible. God help us if this turns into an international manhunt. I presume we're checking out the drugs angle on this. Whoever killed the child in that way must have been high as a bloody kite." She retreated behind her desk and faced her computer. But she wasn't quite finished with him.

"Sam," she said in a low voice, as he got up to follow the others out.

"You should have taken Julie with you. You know the rules."

"Yes, I'll take her with me today," he said. Had Julie complained behind his back? "Sorry, but it was the weekend." It sounded as lame as what he said next. "We'll need help on this, by the way."

* * *

Charlotte Bligh raised her hands and eyes towards heaven. Clayton knew the financial pressures as well as she did. They both also knew that soon she'd have to make recommendations about where to make cuts in the investigation team. If Bligh worked on the basis of last in, first out, it would have to be Julie Everett. She was the most recent addition to the Norwich team. But she had a reputation as an effective and canny detective who'd persist with cases after her other colleagues had given up. So perhaps Neil Pringle would have to go.

So Bligh's strategy for now was to put the screws on Clayton, although she knew he lashed out under pressure. Bligh reasoned that if they were successful in their investigation, they would be less likely to be sacrificed. But who could predict what would happen to policing across the country? Maybe they'd all end up being outsourced and privatised.

"Politicians," she sighed.

* * *

Julie pointed at Neil's hand. "Wife gone for you with the carving knife again?"

"Jealous?" he answered.

Julie flushed. Her jokes never seemed to work.

"Actually, you're not too far off," Neil said. "Except it was me with the carving knife. My thumb got in the way of a leg of lamb yesterday lunchtime. Didn't have time to enjoy it, mind, as I got called out to Glaveny."

"I know," she said, pointedly.

Clayton sat down and stretched his feet out on his desk. "Well, no pressure then."

"Bligh's bark's worse than her bite," Neil said.

"Do you know something we don't?" said Clayton. "Three wives not enough for you?"

Julie didn't smile.

Neil grimaced. "Not my type, actually. Bit too butch for me." He checked his watch and walked out. The others knew that moments later he'd be back with three cups of coffee from the dispenser.

Neil handed round the drinks. "So, do you want me to see the hotel manager?"

"Thanks. Yes. See about family history. We'll get an officer to follow up on the drugs. Julie and I will talk to the dad and Eddie." Clayton paused. He hated tears. There'd been plenty of those when Claire left, and most of them had been his. She'd walked out of his life so coldly, as if he was a shop that no longer stocked her favourite product. In their jobs they both had to keep their emotions under control. But Claire had always had the edge. Nursing was tough.

He picked up a pen and returned to his list. They'd have to start all over again with the same locals who'd been questioned after Jimmy Spratley's death. They all seemed to have something to hide. Farmers feared police investigations into illegally hired migrant workers. And then there was the one-eyed hermit of Pelham-next-the-

Marsh who looked like a villain straight out of central casting. Too obvious.

Clayton looked up at Neil. "Oh, and get whatever you can from the hotel manager on this Frenchman. In Glaveny he'd stand out like a fart in a lift."

"Might be more fragrant than that," Neil said. "Don't they all wear eau de cologne?"

Julie said nothing. She never joined in their boys' banter. "It strikes me that both murders have one thing in common. They weren't murdered on the spot, right? The boy was already dead when he was taken to the churchyard. And the waitress was killed before being taken to the boat."

Clayton twisted round in his chair. "That's what forensics said. It was after she'd finished her lunchtime shift. But what are you driving at?"

"Just wondering whether there might be some connection. It was Halloween. Do you remember that satanist sect that was broken up?" Julie couldn't help noticing that Neil didn't look at her. His eyes were on Clayton when she spoke.

"Those guys who desecrated the graves? Weren't they just some drunken yobs?"

"Yes, but Halloween was only three days ago. A woman dies just days after this killer or killers ripped out a little boy's heart. What if it was some sort of human sacrifice?" Julie said.

"In Glaveny? Don't be ridiculous," Neil said. He was the only one of them to come from Norfolk. Clayton had been promoted to DI from Lancashire and Julie had moved from Ipswich. Neil loved showing off his local knowledge and never missed an opportunity to do so.

Julie pulled a face. "Just saying."

Clayton scratched the back of his ear with his pen. "Okay, never mind the satanists. Let's try good old-fashioned police work. Logic, not superstition." He tried to think. Were both murders carried out on the marsh?

Maybe they had that in common. Were they both premeditated, or was Emma Dawson's killing an opportunistic attack? Either way, he was beginning to think that the child and the waitress were the victims of the same sick killer.

Chapter 4

The trouble with villages is that they're so damned small. Clayton and Julie were on their way back to Glaveny through empty countryside. Give me a big city any day, Clayton thought. Never mind the grime, the noise, all that. People *talk*. And that's how you solve crimes. Glaveny, Branstable, Pelham, all these places scattered about this godforsaken marshland, how can you ever find what they're hiding?

Julie broke into his thoughts. "Left here."

He turned sharply into the cul-de-sac and came to an abrupt halt beside a faded clump of hollyhocks. Their tall stalks lined the street, and like weary sentinels they leaned against the flint-stone. A white forensics van and a patrol car were already parked outside Emma Dawson's cottage.

"Get out of bed on the wrong side today?"

Clayton got out and slammed the door. "Spare me the female intuition."

Outside the cottage, a constable was stamping his feet to keep warm. Julie and Clayton waved to him and knocked at the next door along. As soon as Becky Berry opened the door they heard the sound of a child sobbing. Becky was wiping away her own tears with a tissue.

"Eddie's upstairs with his dad," she said.

Clayton could smell alcohol on her breath. He pointed up the stairs. "May we?"

Becky nodded.

"Is Jack up there too?" he asked.

She sniffed. "He's at school. Best place for him today."

"How old is he?" Julie said.

"He's nine. He's like an older brother to Eddie."

Brian Dawson was slumped on the bed, his arm gripping his son round the shoulders. Eddie's feet hammered against the bed. He didn't look up when the detectives entered.

Julie sat down and reached out for his hand, but he pulled it away. Julie magic's not working today, thought Clayton.

Julie hesitated for a moment, then went downstairs again to ask Becky if she'd sit with Eddie while they spoke with his father.

Dawson followed Clayton down the narrow stairs. He was a heavy-set man who seemed out of place in the low-ceilinged cottage.

"My condolences," said Clayton, shaking his hand and gesturing to a chair. "We're pulling out all the stops."

"I just can't believe it," he said. "Nobody should have to identify a body like that. And I'm worried about Eddie. He won't talk, not even to me. How will he cope with moving to Norwich? He'll miss his friends and all."

"The head teacher will help you with the arrangements," Julie said. "He might need some kind of counselling. They do that for bereaved children. And please tell us if Eddie says anything of interest, the slightest thing. He may have some vital information about what happened."

"He seems to feel guilty about it. At least I think so. Who knows what's going on in that child's mind?"

Clayton took down Dawson's personal details in his notebook. He was a car salesman in Norwich. "When did you last see Eddie and Emma, Mr Dawson?"

He'd last seen Emma about six weeks ago when he'd picked up his son for the weekend.

"And how often did you usually see him?"

"About every six weeks or so." Hardly a hands-on father then, Clayton thought. "My girlfriend and her daughter moved in last year, so it's sometimes a problem finding the time to see my son. I have to work some weekends you see."

"And your partner's name is?"

"Caitlin. And the girl is Lauren."

"Any phone calls from Emma in the days before she was murdered? Did she give any hints that she was worried about anything?"

"We didn't have much contact after the divorce. That was about a year ago. We only ever phoned each other to speak about Eddie, and I wasn't supposed to have him again until just before Christmas."

Becky came downstairs, rubbing her eyes. "You'd better go up. I've got to get ready to pick up my Jack."

Dawson pushed himself up from the armchair.

Becky was rummaging in a cupboard for something. She looked back at Julie and closed the door.

"You driving?" Julie said.

"Walking. It's not far."

* * *

"You'd better make arrangements to talk to Becky Berry's son — you or someone else," said Clayton as they left the house. He zipped up his anorak against the cold.

"Sure," Julie said. Then she look around. "Oh shit."

The cul-de-sac was jammed with cars. The forensics van and the police Vauxhall were now surrounded by reporters. Some were interviewing the neighbours. A constable held them back and lifted the police tape to let his colleagues into Emma Dawson's cottage.

As Clayton slipped on protective gloves and shoe covers, he saw a picture on the living-room wall beside Eddie's drawings. Strange, he hadn't noticed it the day before. It was a painting of a young woman with heavy-lidded blue eyes, wearing a white headdress. "Who do you think that is? Her mother? Emma in fancy dress?"

"Let's see," Julie said, screwing up her eyes. "Isn't it Mother Julian of Norwich?"

"Who?"

"Haven't you heard of her? The medieval mystic. Bats in the belfry."

"Why would Emma have her picture?"

"Beats me. But she's actually got quite a following round here. I'll check it out." Julie went into the kitchen and switched on the light. She began opening cupboards.

"The tap's dripping," she said, turning it off.

Clayton searched the living room. He was aware again of a slight draught, the clamminess in the air. They found no personal items, no diaries. Through the kitchen window they could see the technicians in their white boiler suits sifting through two wheelie bins in the back garden. Clayton knocked on the kitchen window to attract their attention. "Might as well leave this for the techies."

Behind them, the front door opened. "Anyone in?" It was Neil.

"How did you get on at the hotel?" said Clayton.

"You can imagine. The manager's not very happy about his best waitress being murdered. Bad for business after Jimmy Spratley."

"What about the Frenchman?"

"No one's seen him. It's Hampstead-on-sea here. He says they don't get many French. They don't like the weather. And it's a bit out of the way."

Clayton frowned. "So that was worthwhile then."

"Hang on. He gave me the number of a couple from London he saw chatting with Emma. He thought they met up at the Harbour Inn too."

"Okay. Well, let's carry on with the house calls. And we'll start with the pub. It's lunchtime anyway."

Two crime-scene officers came in through the back door carrying plastic bags.

"What've you got, Fiona? Clayton felt sorry for the dour scientist every time he spoke to her. Was she aware that the entire force knew her as Fifi? The playful nickname kind of humanised her.

"We've taken some samples from the kitchen, the bed, carpet fibres, the usual."

"Computer?"

"No sign of one," she said. "But we found the victim's phone in the mac she was wearing in the boat."

Clayton went to the front window and looked out. He checked both sides of the street but couldn't see what he was looking for.

Fiona intercepted his glance. "No CCTV I'm afraid. There's not even any street lighting."

Clayton and Julie pushed through the journalists and drove to the Harbour Inn, followed by Neil. All conversation stopped dead as the three new arrivals entered the bar. Clayton noticed the 'duck or grouse' sign just in time.

He motioned to Julie to find seats while he and Neil ordered at the bar. The customers were mostly male, some in work overalls, others in jeans. Everyone was staring at them. Even the couple of tourists looked up from their maps. It was so quiet Clayton could hear the clock ticking.

He began to drum his fingers on the bar. Just as they were about to give up, the barmaid moved along to them, her dangly earrings swaying amid the waves of her Norfolk ginger hair.

Clayton spoke in a low voice, aware of everyone in the pub listening to him. "Anglian Constabulary Major Investigation Team." He showed her his warrant card.

"You're here about Emma then," the barmaid said loudly.

Neil took out his notebook, wrote something down and passed it across the bar.

"We need to talk to you. Call this number, please." He picked up his half pint of Adnams and took an orange juice over to Julie.

The barmaid stage-whispered to Clayton that she was alone behind the bar. She would see them outside after her shift.

Chapter 5

Julie left her colleagues in the pub. At a brisk pace it would take her about fifteen minutes to walk up to St Nicholas church. She was following a hunch. The vicar, who'd discovered the body, hadn't helped them shed any light on Jimmy Spratley's murder. But it was always worth a second try.

The door of the medieval guildhall was open. It was dark and empty inside, and she caught a whiff of urine as she walked past. She had no time to browse in the gift shops on the High Street, or to study the restaurant menus. The village was eerily quiet after the half term holiday. Looking through windows, she guessed that many of the empty houses were second homes. Some cottages had holiday rental signs posted on doors and windowsills. A row of squishy pumpkins stood outside the village hall, which was still decorated with fake spiders' webs.

She reached the main road and turned towards the church whose tall tower dominated the endless landscape.

She was in luck. She saw the vicar, a tall figure with an Old Testament grey beard, shaking hands with a woman. As the detective walked up to the entrance, her eyes were drawn to the mound of soil by the stone wall, draped with police tape. Pots of chrysanthemums and bunches of flowers were piled beside Jimmy Spratley's grave. On the far side of the graveyard was the primary school where he'd been a pupil.

"Excuse me . . . er, sir," she said as the vicar went back into the church. She realised she didn't know how to address a vicar. He turned round. Only the dog collar gave him away.

"DS Julie Everett," she said.

"Ah," he replied. "You've come about the boy again." He indicated a pew at the back of the church, and she sat down. "I've already told you everything I know. I walked across from the vicarage and there it was, in the graveyard. Ever since those satanic rituals, I've made a point of inspecting the graves whenever I'm in the parish." He added, "I have five, you see, in my little empire."

She nodded. "Did you hear about the waitress' body being found at Branstable? The one from the Point Hotel?"

"Do you know Glaveny, Detective Sergeant?"

"Yes. Quite well, I suppose. I've been coming here for years, doing the seal trips, walking the marshes, that sort of thing."

"Well, there's *evil* here."

He was so close to her she could feel his breath on her cheek. She pulled back. "You mean, what happened to the boy?"

He nodded. "But that's not all. You know about the satanists, but have you heard of Black Shuck?"

"You mean the big black dog that roams the marshes? But that's just a legend."

His voice bounced back from the vaulted ceiling. "You think it's a legend? There are parishioners of mine who've seen it come out of the mist. It's evil, I tell you." He leaned towards her and fixed his dark eyes on hers.

"But what do you mean — evil?"

"I'm telling you, things happen when Black Shuck is about."

"Reverend — sir, what proof do you have of that?"

He scratched his beard, thick as a bird's nest. "Proof? Do you know about all the dead pets in the village? They didn't die from disease or old age. But you won't get anybody here to tell you. They don't talk to strangers. In the five years I've been in this parish, I've had to re-consecrate the graveyard twice. That poor boy . . . and St Nicholas is supposed to be the protector of children." He stared at the embroidered flowers on the prayer cushion in front of him.

Julie tried again. "Do you think the satanists had anything to do with Emma Dawson, the waitress? Did you know her?"

The vicar picked up the prayer cushion and began stroking the floral pattern.

"Yes. She would come in to talk. She was interested in Mother Julian and believed she had a connection to the parish. You've heard of the Mother?"

"Of course. She was around in medieval times. But I don't know much about her."

"Let's say she was unorthodox. She was a mystic, of course, but I would say within the Catholic tradition. Essentially, in the struggle between good and evil, she was on the side of the angels. 'All shall be well, and all shall be well, and all manner of thing shall be well.'"

"Is that something she said?"

He nodded. "That's one of the Mother's best known sayings from her *Revelations of Divine Love*. But most people forget, or aren't aware, that before she said 'all shall be well' she said that 'sin is inevitable.'"

The vicar lowered his voice to a confiding whisper. "She wrote a lot about sin. She said that sin is *behovely* — necessary. And that, in turn, brings us to seek God's forgiveness."

Julie took out her notebook and wrote down the reference.

"There's another thing she wrote in the same vein. Just bear with me while I get it." He set down the cushion, stood up and went to the back of the church, jingling a set of keys. She saw him opening a locked cupboard and running his finger along a row of books. He came back with a slim volume, his footsteps ringing on the stone floor.

He leant against the pew and flicked through the pages. "Here we are. Listen to this: 'We need to fall, and we need to be aware of it, for if we did not fall, we should not know how weak and wretched we are of ourselves, nor should we know our Maker's marvellous love so fully.' Consider that, Detective. *We need to fall.* You'd do well to remember that in your investigation."

Julie wondered what Clayton would make of all this. She cleared her throat.

"So was Emma religious?"

"Not in the traditional Christian sense, but who is, these days? But she had faith and a fervour, yes, particularly when talking about the Mother. I suppose it's possible that Mother Julian came here from Norwich, although it was a long journey in those days. We think she came to St Andrews, up the road. There's a picture of her there."

Julie made a note to check, wondering where all of this was leading.

The vicar continued. "She might well have come here. The dates certainly coincide. This church was built when she was alive, and of course there was a friary next door. Let me show you something else." He moved towards the choir stalls. She picked up her things and followed him down the aisle.

"Look at these." He indicated the wooden carvings on the stalls. Julie moved closer to examine them. She could make out medieval figures among the motifs. A man's face peeked out from oak leaves. They looked pagan to her.

"Misericords. They have shelves so that the faithful could lean against them for comfort while praying. These are four of the original stalls." He drew her attention to one of them. "Ms Dawson said that she saw a similarity with the vases of flowers in the picture of Mother Julian at Langham. But as you might say, where's the proof?"

"Do you mind if I take a photograph?"

"Of course not."

As she leaned closer, Julie could see quite clearly the motif of two daisies whose stalks were intertwined. It was identical to the tattoo on the dead woman's ankle.

Chapter 6

Clayton and Julie pulled up outside the nature reserve visitors' centre at Branstable Quay just as two wardens were locking up and heading for the jetty.

"We're just going out to rescue some seal pups. You can come with us if you like," said the taller of the two, who introduced himself as Bob Jarvis.

Julie looked doubtfully at Clayton. "I don't mind waiting here," she said. Clayton noticed the yellow police tape clinging to the boat which Emma Dawson's body had been found in. It was only a few yards away from the visitor centre.

"It won't take long," said Jarvis.

"Sure, why not?" said Clayton with a grin. "As long as we're not expected to help you."

The four of them climbed into a grey dinghy. "I'm Mike Skipper," said the younger man, shaking hands.

"So what're we doing exactly?" Clayton asked as the engine sprang into life and they bounced against the wind towards the seal colony.

"We're meeting a guy from the RSPCA on the Point because some of the pups have got separated from their mothers," said Jarvis.

They beached the boat and the two detectives waited in the cold. The seal rescuer was already on the shingle in a pair of waders.

"You ready?" he called out to the wardens. He approached a seal pup barking on the shingle and picked it up by the tail.

"Let's go!" Then, "Watch out, behind you!" Clayton caught sight of a blubbery seal rolling towards the younger warden, who spun round.

"Can you pick up the others?" said the seal rescuer.

Jarvis was the first to step forward, and with a practised hand he swept up a cream-coloured pup, then another, holding them upside down. "These are only a few days old," he said.

Skipper grabbed two others, his gloved hands lifting them like furry toys. They splashed into the waves and dropped the speckled bodies gently into cages on the RSPCA boat.

The man in waders pointed out one that was bleeding through its silvery fur. "This one's injured. I'll take him back to East Winch to get him checked out. The others can go back to their mummies."

"Good job, guys!" He waved from his boat, heading off to reunite the baby seals with their mothers, which were barking in distress.

"I told you it wouldn't take long," Jarvis said as the wardens returned to their dinghy. "Although sometimes it takes longer when the other seals get in the way."

"That was fun," said Clayton.

"They're gorgeous," said Julie.

A few minutes later they were back at the visitor centre, a modest wooden cabin next to the jetty, with an upstairs viewing platform over the marsh.

"Just give us a moment, Inspector, while we take our wellies off," said Jarvis, undoing the lock. He was of muscular build with a shaven head. Skipper followed him inside, smoothing down the blonde tufts of his salt-caked hair.

They beckoned Clayton and Julie into the warm.

"Right, so how can we help you?" said Jarvis.

Clayton asked if they'd come across the Frenchman who'd been seen in Glaveny.

Jarvis fiddled with a pair of binoculars on the counter. "Actually, I did. He came to see me here. Michel was his name, I think."

"Do you happen to know where he's from?"

"Across the Channel," said Jarvis with a straight face. "Sorry, I mean the Somme estuary. It's called St Valéry-sur-Somme. The only reason I'd heard of it is because they've got a seal sanctuary there too. He was telling me about what they're doing there to protect the seals, and they see Glaveny as a model. The reserve here is a hundred years old, so we've got a bit of experience."

"How did he strike you? What was he like physically?"

"Slim, bit shorter than me. Three-day beard. Spoke English quite well."

"Anything else?"

"Maybe a bit shifty?"

Jarvis said he thought the Frenchman had been staying at a bed and breakfast in Glaveny. Shouldn't be too hard to find, thought Clayton. Most of them had closed for the season.

"You been out this morning?" Julie said.

Jarvis put down the binoculars. "No, not till we went out with you to rescue the seal pups. "

"Were either of you out on the day the waitress was killed?" Clayton asked.

Skipper looked up. "When was that exactly?"

"Saturday afternoon. It was misty that day. We think the body was brought right here that same night," Julie said.

Jarvis pulled open a drawer and took out a diary. "We keep a record of all our movements in here. Let's see . . .

Saturday. The information centre is only open part time at the moment. We shut the Lifeboat House at the end of September and stopped full time activities then."

He turned the pages. "I'd been out early to count the wigeons. There's been some duck hunting going on, and the wildfowlers like a particular pond on the marsh."

"Have you seen anything, or anyone, suspicious?" Clayton asked.

Jarvis shook his head. "A couple of walkers maybe, with their dogs. But the weather that morning was atrocious. I didn't stick around long and came back here. I was back by ten."

"May I?" Clayton held out his hand for the book. Saturday's entry read, 'BJ — wigeons.' On the previous day, they had recorded 'MS — dune fencing repair'.

"What's BJ and MS?" asked Clayton. "Is that you?"

"Yes, Bob Jarvis and Mike Skipper," said the older warden.

The previous day's entry was: 'BJ and MS redshank count — 6'. They didn't record exact times. They'd already noted that day's activities as '6 seal pups rescued.'

Julie was staring at the entry for 'dune fencing repair.'

"So what sort of fences were you mending?" she asked Skipper. It struck her that either of them could have easily overcome a twenty-six-year-old woman.

"Wire mesh and wooden posts," he said. "We might have some here." He reached behind the counter and pulled out a coil of fencing. Not barbed wire.

"And what about the Saturday afternoon?"

"I shut up shop here and went into Holt. There was a bit of fret. You were at home, weren't you, mate? You weren't feeling well."

"Yes, that's right." Jarvis paused. "Had a migraine."

Julie remembered that her son Ollie had talked about his school trip to the marshes. "Aren't you involved in educational activities with the schoolkids? Did you know the dead boy at all?"

"Jimmy Spratley? Is that the name? I don't recall him," said Jarvis. "But yes, we have classes come to the information centre. Sometimes we give talks up the road at the school too. I've taken them out bird watching in the marsh, and showed them some tern eggs. The kids got quite excited about that."

"What about Emma Dawson? Did you know her?"

"Oh yes," said Skipper. "I was just going to mention. She was a volunteer seal monitor. Helped us count the pups, that sort of thing. It's getting to be the busiest time of year right now. Nice woman. What a tragedy."

The wardens turned back to the photos.

* * *

The two detectives returned to their car. "They were helpful," said Clayton.

"Yes. Maybe too helpful." Julie looked back towards the centre. It was high tide and the fishing-boat cables were clanking in the muddy channels.

"What do you mean?"

"Just a feeling. Everyone in the village is pointing fingers at this French guy. I mean, fancy calling him shifty, it's just too easy."

"What more do you want, Julie? I reckon it's time to get Europol on the case," said Clayton. "Shouldn't be that hard to find a guy named Michel involved in seal protection in a place on the Somme estuary."

"Don't you want to hear what I found out?"

"Oh aye. The vicar. Tell me." He switched off the ignition.

"He might know more than he lets on. Take a look at this picture for starters." She held up her smartphone.

"My God! The tattoo."

"Emma seems to have been a 'follower' of Mother Julian. And the vicar thinks there might to be a link to Black Shuck. *And* he was talking about pets going missing in the vicinity."

Clayton banged his hand on the steering wheel. "Nonsense, Julie. We want facts, not silly superstitions."

"I've just got you one, haven't I?"

"Okay, so Emma had a thing about Mother Julian. I don't see where that gets us."

He started the car again and they set off. Julie stared out of the window at the flint houses as they drove.

"Well, what did you and Neil find out then?" Julie swallowed the "smart-arse" that had been on the tip of her tongue.

"The barmaid saw Emma with the Frenchman in the pub on Thursday night. Apparently they hooked up because of their mutual interest in seals."

"And how did the barmaid know that?"

"The two women have been friends since their schooldays."

"So, Thursday night. That's two days before she went missing."

"Correct. Bingo!" said Clayton, checking the rear mirror.

"And the motive?"

"Why do you have to always spoil everything, Julie?"

Chapter 7

Clayton dreamed of a child with a hole where his heart should have been. He took off his airline mask and peered at the clock. It was only 6.30 a.m.

He shut his eyes tight. It occurred to him that he'd have time for his favourite run at Holkham beach if he got up now. But it was an hour's drive from his terraced house in Norwich. He sighed, sat up straight, fumbled in a pile of laundry on a chair for his running gear and went downstairs.

This place is too big for me, he thought, as he headed past the empty spare bedrooms. He and Claire had bought it planning to have children. He'd be better off with a two-bedroom house. He had this thought every day. Claire had been gone for more than a year and all the guitar music in the world wasn't going to replace her. So many songs had gone with her — Neil Young, Eric Clapton, Paul McCartney. He'd only played them to please her anyway. He'd always preferred the classical guitar. Nobody else in Clayton's family was musical, unless you counted his father singing on the terraces at Preston North End.

He remembered the moment when he'd first heard a guitar. One evening after tea, the family was in the living room as usual — his younger sister was arguing with their mother and Clayton was just waiting for the moment when Melanie would get what she wanted. His dad switched on the radio and Clayton's attention was caught by a strange rasping, along with the purest sound he'd ever heard. He had stood with his ear to the radio and told them all to shut up, while he listened with his eyes closed. He'd never experienced such tranquillity.

They told him it was Julian Bream at the Proms. And he didn't even have to ask for a guitar — it appeared on his bed a few months later, on his seventeenth birthday. Maybe his parents had thought it would keep him from fighting with Melanie. Well, it had worked.

He'd met Claire in Manchester where he'd been a beat bobby. One night he became the target of some overexcited lads using beer bottles to play skittles outside a pub. She'd treated him at the Royal Infirmary.

"Were they using you for target practice?" were the first words she spoke to him. She was bandaging his head with the gentlest fingers he'd ever felt. The image of Claire wearing one of his T-shirts, her head cocked to one side, stayed in his mind as he drove to the coast, Classic FM turned down low. He regretted that neither of them had fought to keep the marriage alive, even as they drifted towards what became an inevitable split after the move to Norwich. She said he'd changed when his career began to take off. He'd retreat to an upstairs bedroom, to practise with the door closed, while she watched TV downstairs among the furnishings she'd chosen. They'd only just invested in a new beige sofa when she moved out.

Was he to blame? She'd accused him of bottling things up, but they were both too busy to rake over the embers of their dying relationship.

He parked the VW in the car park at the entrance to the beach. It sat there surrounded by empty spaces. He'd never been to Holkham so early before. The morning air was still but the pines were whispering when he reached the dunes. He could just see a faint glimmer of light at the horizon.

He filled his lungs, admiring the shades of blue, green and yellow that stretched out before him. He'd forgotten how magical Holkham could be. There wasn't a soul in sight — too cold for the naturists at this time of year. His trainers pounded the hard sand as he ran out towards the white line of the sea margin. He should run more often. It helped him work off his pent-up frustrations, bottled-up emotions, his rage.

The owners of the bed and breakfast in Glaveny had told the police that the man known as Michel Billard had left on Sunday morning. Emma was killed the previous afternoon. The timing fit, he thought. The post-mortem had shown that she'd had sex around two days before she died. But *why* would he have killed her?

Oh God, I'm sounding like Julie Everett, he thought. Her and her motive. Well, if it wasn't the Frenchman, who was it then? He was breathing more heavily now, feeling the impact on his knees. All right. She was a waitress. Had they concentrated enough on that angle? They'd have to contact all the hotel guests who'd stayed at the Point over the preceding days. Maybe there was something they had overlooked. It had to be someone she knew.

Then there were the Glaveny eccentrics, and there were plenty of those. The 'hermit of Pelham' for a start, who wandered in the marshes with his dog. But everyone said he was harmless. Could Emma have had a chance encounter that turned sour? Lots of people would have met her at the hotel, or the pub, or even out on the marsh. Then there were the farmhands, and the migrant workers.

Clayton's list of potential suspects grew with every stride. Any number of people might have crossed paths with the Glaveny waitress. What about an appeal for witnesses? What about the wardens? Why was Julie suspicious of them? Might they have seen something on their patrols that they were keeping to themselves?

He remembered the travellers who camped on the outskirts of Glaveny. They were rarely seen in the village but there'd been some thefts reported, which had never been solved. Emma must have been garrotted on the marsh. But why? Who was this woman really?

He turned back, panting and disconsolate, to the car park. His mind was still churning. They still had no idea whether there was a link between the two deaths. And what about the missing pets? Julie had been right — two cats and a spaniel had been reported missing by their owners in the weeks before Jimmy's body was discovered. They'd never been found.

Then there was Emma's ex. They'd arranged to interview him at the police station. Julie was supposed to be speaking to the parents. Clayton stretched and kicked out at a green rubbish bin, Bruce Lee style, startling a group of seagulls fighting over a crust of bread.

* * *

Police headquarters was a glass-and-brick building resembling a spaceship, supposedly it was a fine example of modern architecture. Clayton could see its squat shape from more than a mile away after turning off the Norwich ring road and heading west. It sat in isolation as though it had crash-landed in a remote field. The force had moved into the new premises because of the merger. He'd never known the old nick in the city, but colleagues told him that they missed it because it had been so much more convenient for cafes and pubs. Now they were stuck with the office cafeteria.

Bligh was waiting for him with that morning's *Eastern Daily Press*. She threw it across his desk. The front page headline read, 'French Drifter Sought in Glaveny Waitress Murder.' French drifter! Where had they got that line from?

"What's this?" she said. "Where does this nonsense in the EDP come from? It's all over Twitter. I checked with the press office and they told me that they'd kept to the facts and told reporters that the body of a Glaveny waitress had been found and that investigations were continuing."

Clayton wondered whether Bligh could hear the sounds coming from his empty stomach.

"This can only have come from your team," she said. "Tipping off a suspect! Whatever next!"

"Give me a minute. I'll find out," he said to Bligh's back. "But what they don't know is that as soon as he's been positively identified we're going to France before you can say 'Allo, 'Allo."

He called in Julie and Neil. Neil looked sheepish. "I think this might have come from me. Sorry."

"From you?"

"I *might* have mentioned to the hotel manager that we were looking for a Frenchman. I *might* have said drifter, I don't remember. And of course the hotel guy talked to the media. I'm sorry."

"Okay. Well, don't do it again. The last thing we need is the French press showing up in Glaveny as well. We can't have people thinking we have a suspect before we've even interviewed him."

He waved them away. He urgently wanted to go down to the canteen to pick up something to eat, but then he noticed a Post-it message stuck to his phone. Pandora Delingpole had left a message. She was the customer from the Point Hotel who'd talked to Emma. He rang her number.

"How can I help you, Inspector? We've heard that the nice waitress from the Point Hotel has been killed. We're in complete shock."

"We understand that a Frenchman was in Glaveny over the weekend. If there's anything you think might help us, please let me know."

"What, is he a suspect?"

"I can't say, Mrs Delingpole. Did he already know Emma? And do you know where he was going after Glaveny?"

"I'm afraid I don't know. Emma told us they met on a boat trip to check the seals. I don't think he knew Emma previously. We saw him on a boat trip too, he was taking notes and pictures. Then we saw him again at the pub on Thursday night."

"Which pub?"

"I'm afraid I can't remember the name. You go out of the hotel and turn left . . ."

"You mean the Harbour Inn?"

"Yes, that's right. Of course. He drew us a map on a napkin connecting Glaveny to the place he comes from. They've got a seal colony there too, and he said it's the biggest in France."

"Could you describe him?"

"Average height, late twenties. Unshaven. No, a beard. You know — that designer stubble. He wore an anorak and a baggy green jumper. Hiking boots. He carried a backpack."

"Hair colour?"

"Let me see . . . dark, I think. Wavy. Longer than people wear it here. He had jeans on, but everybody does, don't they?"

"Anything else?"

"I'm afraid not, although I do remember he was frightfully attractive. Actually we left in a bit of a hurry on Saturday morning."

Clayton waited.

"We had a bit of a scare. Silly, really."

"What do you mean?" He took his feet off the desk and leaned forward.

"Have you heard of Black Shuck? The hound that some people say prowls in the marshes at night? Well, I think we saw it, and it scared us to death!"

"Where?"

"In the marshes. It came out of the reed beds, and it was huge. It was moving like in slow motion and its eyes were big as saucers. Honestly, Inspector, I've never seen anything like it!"

Clayton tapped his foot in irritation. Not this superstitious nonsense again. "What happened?"

"It passed right in front of us, its long red tongue was hanging out, and it disappeared into the mist. We went running back to the hotel and got our things together straight away."

"Thank you, Mrs Delingpole. Most helpful." Clayton slammed the phone back onto its cradle.

He was still staring at it when Julie came in.

"What's the matter?" she said. "You look like you've seen a ghost."

"Well, someone did: the posh couple from the hotel who went to the pub with Emma and met the Frenchman. She says they saw Black Shuck on Saturday morning. Another shaggy dog story."

"Wait a sec!" Julie said. "Black Shuck? Don't you know about the devil hound? It's important here in East Anglia, people really believe in it. Ask Neil. I read that they found the bones of one near a ruined abbey in Suffolk only a few months ago. What if it was Black Shuck that dug up the boy's heart?"

"Where I come from, we don't do devil dogs," he said with a grin.

"Well, round here they say that when you see Black Shuck it means you're going to die. Or that there will be a death. The vicar told me bad things happen when it's about. If they saw it on Saturday morning, and Emma died on the Saturday afternoon, maybe there's a connection."

"Connection my arse," he said. "Mrs Delingpole seems to have survived the encounter. Christ, Julie, this is a murder investigation, not a séance."

Julie folded her arms. "Well, listen to this. Actually we are talking about séances. I just spoke to Emma's parents and it turns out that she was some kind of psychic medium. She was doing Ouija board stuff when she was still young. She started out with Tarot cards and then she got a thing about Mother Julian. They said she was in touch with Emma from beyond the grave."

Chapter 8

The fishermen of Saint-Valéry-sur-Somme were jammed into the meeting hall, cheering every speaker who rose to demand the culling of the seals.

"We're going to take this to Brussels!" shouted a bearded speaker who commanded attention from his seat in the middle of the room. Michel Billard recognised him, he'd come from a port further along the coast. Billard hoped he wouldn't be noticed with his fellow seal protector, Jean-Pierre Rossignol, standing at the back of the room. He looked around furtively. There were about twenty fishermen and a few wildfowlers too.

"We're fighting for our livelihoods here! One seal eats five kilos of fish every day. And another thing — they destroy our nets, and who's going to pay for that?" The speaker was now on his feet.

Sensing the mood in the hall, he moved towards the front.

"90,000 people now support us," he said to more applause. Billard and Rossignol exchanged glances and raised their eyebrows.

"We're supported by fishermen's associations from as far away as Norway and even Canada. And England too!"

As he droned on, Billard's thoughts turned to Glaveny. He remembered the girl, Emma, and her passion when she'd talked about the seals on the boat trip where they'd first met. Her softness, her English complexion and her smooth white neck. Their two nights together, trying to be as quiet as possible, buried under the bedclothes, while her son slept in the room next door. He was a strange little boy, who'd recoiled when they first met and he'd held out his hand in greeting. Billard smiled to himself. Maybe he'd never met a foreigner before.

But then it had got complicated. Emma hadn't wanted him to stay for breakfast, and he'd crept out like a thief at daybreak, holding his boots in his hand. He'd felt humiliated. She said she didn't want her son to know he'd spent the night. How was he to know that she already had a boyfriend? He frowned.

The fisherman was still talking. Billard glanced at his companion. They were supposed to report back to the association about this meeting. They didn't want to get involved in a slanging match with the fishermen, they were bound to lose. Billard motioned to the door. A couple of minutes later, as the speaker was reading out the numbers of seal pups born in the colony that summer, they sidled along the back wall and left.

They settled down to a couple of beers on a nearby café terrace and Rossignol lit up a cigarette. "So tell me about your trip."

"They say it's now the biggest seal colony in Britain. Ours is the biggest in France, but you'd never guess. They told me that in Glaveny they would never cull seals. You can see hundreds of them on the Point there. But here . . ." He pressed a fist into his other palm.

Rossignol exhaled. His nicotine-stained fingers showed the nicks of the carpenter's trade. "When you were away last week, the wankers took a boat out and stood there with a banner saying 'Enough is Enough.' They're all over the media."

"Bastards."

"The thing is, it's the tourists who are in love with the seals, not the people of St Valéry."

"That may be, but at least the fishermen could talk to us about it. A proper meeting so we can thrash things out. If not, things are going to get out of hand." Billard got up, searching in his pocket for some spare change, and waited while Rossignol stubbed out his cigarette.

That night, from his bedsit opposite the old *gendarmerie*, Billard was woken by a crack of gunfire.

Its staccato sound punctuated the nights during the hunting season. To Billard it was a form of torture. After waking, he would lie and wait for the next volley to be fired. Just as he was falling back to sleep another burst of gunfire made him jump.

The wildfowlers were close by in their covered hides, near the ponds they dug to attract ducks and migrating birds. The birds were literally sitting ducks for the shooters concealed in the hides. Billard got up and poured himself a glass of water. He'd had a few run-ins with the hunters, a couple of punch-ups. At this time of year, they were hard to avoid. It wouldn't be long until dawn. He shut the window and went back to bed just as a fresh volley rang out.

* * *

After a breakfast of coffee and a *tartine,* Billard took the river walk through the town centre and scanned the waters for the dark heads of seals. It was high tide. He always took his binoculars with him, just in case, but he knew there was only a slight chance he'd see one. He took a short cut through the mini-golf and strolled along a path lined by horse chestnuts and lime trees. His scarf fluttered in the north wind. He went into the job centre. He needed to plan ahead. If he could find work over Christmas, he'd have enough to survive.

He reached the newsagent, whose window was full of guidebooks on local sights. But what he noticed was the headline in the Courrier Picard on the newspaper stand outside:

> Police hunt St Valéry man for murder in England.

He went inside and picked up a paper. His heart raced as he read to the end of the article. What was this? There was his name in black and white. Emma looked so young and pretty in the photo. Her oval face, framed by brown hair, looked straight at him from the page. She was smiling. His hands began to tremble as he turned the page, and he fought down the urge to flee. At least his picture wasn't in the paper. A couple of tourists were leafing through calendars. He had to wait to pay behind two other people who were chatting about a reality TV star who was on the cover of their magazine. He took his woolly hat out of his jacket pocket and put it on. He paid with his face lowered, almost forgetting his change, and rushed out of the shop without speaking.

He needed to think. He walked back along the High Street, past the fish restaurants, bistros and crêperies. The menu boards had disappeared — they'd finally taken their tables and chairs inside with the end of the mild weather and most were closed during the day. He kept on past the gift shop where they sold bird ornaments and furry toy seals. He crossed the square and walked past his flat into the old town. He went through the medieval archway, past the church, through the square and up to the perfect roundness of the towers of the stone fortress. He reached the lookout point and stood, admiring the vast bay below. It was one of his favourite spots in St Valéry.

He needed to disappear. But where could he go? He had hardly any money in the bank so he couldn't travel far. They'd be looking for him anyway. At least he had a head start. The flat where he was staying wasn't in his name. The police wouldn't know that he was subletting it from a friend who was seal watching in Scotland for a couple of months.

He stared out over the grey-green marshes. Then his phone rang. Fearing the worst, he checked the caller. It was Rossignol.

"Have you seen the paper? You know you're wanted for murder?"

Billard pulled down his hat further over his ears and raised his jacket collar. "I just read it."

There was a short silence. "Are you going to the police?"

"I don't know. You don't think I killed the girl, do you?" He didn't recognise his own voice. He hadn't meant to growl.

"Of course not. Why would you? But why are they after you?"

"I know as much as you do."

"Where are you?"

"At the Joan of Arc gate." The two of them always called it that. She'd been imprisoned by the English in the fortress before they took her to Rouen and burned her at the stake. Now the English are looking for me, Billard thought. What will they do to me?

"Wait for me, I'll be there in ten minutes."

Billard was still standing by the stone wall, looking across the estuary, when Rossignol arrived pushing his bike. Billard was thinking about Emma. She had heard voices too, like Joan. After putting her son to bed she'd sat with the black cat on her lap, and held his hands. He'd watched her contact the spirit world. She'd trembled in his hands, her eyes wide open while she listened to her dead mother. At the end she'd said, meekly, "Yes, Mother." He shivered at the memory.

On the other side of the estuary the low skyline of Le Crotoy was backlit by the sun. A bank of clouds, dark and bloated, inched across the big sky.

"What are you going to do?" said Rossignol quietly. Two other men had arrived at the lookout, carrying binoculars. Billard and Rossignol looked at each other. The newcomers spoke in low grunts and were obviously watching the tide. But they weren't speaking in French. Was it English? One of the men was French, but the other was definitely foreign. Whatever language it was, it had a heavy accent.

They remained silent as their two neighbours raised their binoculars again and began talking excitedly as a boat came into view. Billard picked up his binoculars too and focussed on the boat. It wasn't a fishing boat. And it was full of people.

Four pairs of binoculars were now trained on the boat. They could almost hear the sound of its outboard motor, carried by the breeze. But instead of floating along the river to the town marina, it turned along a channel between the mud-banks. The two strangers went down the steps from the lookout. They seemed to be in a hurry.

Billard and Rossignol watched them push aside the undergrowth until they disappeared from sight, then turned their binoculars back to the boat. Its passengers, all men, disembarked and began walking across the salt marsh in single file.

"What was that do you think?" Billard asked. "Why didn't they moor the boat in the marina?"

"Didn't you hear?" said Rossignol. "It's the people trafficking. They come along here now to try to get to England. Too many problems in Calais. Some of us have been tipping off the cops."

"What? You're an informer?" Billard's heart began to pound.

"I wouldn't call it that. I'm a citizen doing my duty. What's wrong with that?"

"So are you going to tell them about what we just saw?"

"I don't know. Might do. We don't want them here."

They sat down on a bench overlooking the bay. Billard had decided what to do. He wouldn't hand himself in and he couldn't involve his friend, particularly in the light of what he'd just said.

"I've been thinking," he said. "I'm going to lay low for a while. Let things blow over."

Rossignol looked at him sharply. "Where are you going?"

"I don't want to get you involved," he said. "What if they contact you?"

"Well, keep in touch," said Rossignol.

Billard nodded and they shook hands. He headed back to his bedsit. There was no time to lose. He opened the fridge, which was empty apart from a couple of beer bottles and a rancid bottle of milk. He stowed the beer in a backpack along with some clothes.

Inside a kitchen drawer was his prized Laguiole pocket knife, a gift from his parents. Who knows, he thought, this might come in handy. He opened the steel blade and felt the weight in the palm of his hand. He admired the knife's marbled cow-horn handle. He'd skinned rabbits with this in the past. People didn't realise how easy it was, the skin peeled back cleanly in seconds. He folded the knife again and slipped it into his pocket. Then he rooted out his small tent from the back of a cupboard and locked up, slamming the door behind him.

Checking the street for cars and people, still wearing his hat pulled down over his ears, he went to the nearest ATM. He tapped in his code and chose a withdrawal of 200 euros, the maximum allowed on his account. The machine responded with 'unauthorised transaction.'

He thought there must be some mistake. He tried again, but the same message popped up on the screen. He typed in 100 euros, and received the same reply. His account had been blocked. Was it the police? He didn't dare try again. He screwed his eyes up, staring at the screen and tried to remember when he'd last used the card. He realised it must have been the bed and breakfast in Glaveny that had pushed his account into the red. He swore under his breath. The charity was supposed to reimburse him for his travel expenses, but he'd had to pay upfront.

Or was it the police? He glanced up and down the street while he waited to retrieve his card, but saw no one except two customers coming out of the fishmongers.

He only had fifteen euros on him.

He went to the bus stop where he counted down the twelve minutes he had to wait, poised to take flight if necessary. When the bus finally trundled along, he stood in the space reserved for pushchairs, scanning the faces of the elderly passengers. The driver dropped him outside the town at a roundabout near a McDonalds. He hiked down the hill to the campsite a couple of kilometres away. The season was over and only a few scattered caravans and caravans were dotted around the site. He should be able to find a secluded spot where nobody would notice him.

He was sweating by the time he reached the entrance. The gates were closed. He carried on until he reached a wooden gate. He flung his things over it and climbed into a remote section of the campsite behind some empty cabins. With a bit of luck, he'd be safe here for a while.

Chapter 9

Emma Dawson's mother leaned on her husband for support as Julie guided them into an interview room.

"Thanks so much again for your help, Mr and Mrs Onslow. We're trying to build up a picture of your daughter, and I just want to follow up on what you said on the phone."

Both of them had dressed formally for the meeting. Rita Onslow, a small woman with eyes red from crying, sat up straight as if preparing for the first question.

"What went wrong with her marriage?" Julie began.

Mr Onslow let his wife answer. His eyes were half-closed as though he was sleepwalking.

Mrs Onslow sighed. "It was a bit one-sided in my view," she said, twisting her wedding ring. "Brian loved Eddie of course, but he was always a bit hands-off. They had some money worries as well, what with the recession, and I think Brian wasn't getting as much commission as before."

"Commission? At the car showroom?"

The woman nodded.

"But was there something in particular that led to the marriage breakdown?"

"Who knows what goes on inside a marriage?"

"Brian Dawson wasn't violent, was he?"

Mrs Onslow leaned forward. "Oh no! Nothing like that. He was quite passive actually. He'd never hit anyone, and with Eddie he left all the discipline to Emma. She ended up doing everything."

Her husband nodded.

"Were you involved in the childcare at all?"

"She always had help from her neighbours, when she was in Norwich and when she moved back to Glaveny. She was such a friendly girl, everyone wanted to help her."

Someone didn't, Julie thought.

Rita Onslow reached inside her handbag for a tissue. "Who could have done this to our lovely girl? Only a month before her twenty-seventh birthday! It's not supposed to be like this, is it? Children going before their parents."

Julie switched off the tape recorder and waited. Onslow patted his wife's hand. Then she resumed. "She had a brother, is that right?"

Mrs Onslow said that Emma's younger brother worked in Cornwall as a surfing instructor.

"Can you tell me about her spiritualist tendencies? The séances and everything."

Mr Onslow cast a quick glance at his wife. "We never approved of her spiritual activities."

"Why's that then?"

"We never had anything to do with it, of course. It started out as a bit of fun when she was at school. But after she left and started work, she came under the influence of an evangelical group, some kind of sect. The leader was an older man and we think they had a relationship, don't we, Rita?"

Mrs Onslow had recovered somewhat. "Most definitely. Because when he dropped her, she had some kind of breakdown. That's when she became obsessed with Mother Julian."

"What kind of breakdown? Was she hospitalised?"

The couple looked at each other before Mr Onslow spoke. "She was for a bit, yes, and they gave her some pills."

"And when you say she became obsessed with Mother Julian, was that before or after her hospitalisation?"

"Before. Definitely before. I blame that man. He changed her, he really did."

His wife sighed. "Yes. She was completely under the influence of that man. He was always ringing her, asking her to do stuff. She was different when she was with him. She became like him. She'd boast about being in touch with Mother Julian, that sort of thing. We didn't see too much of her then, I can tell you."

"Can you remember his name? Do you know what happened to him?"

"What was his name, dear?"

Mr Onslow shrugged his shoulders. "Robert something I think. But he's dead now, he got run over. I read about it in the paper. To tell you the truth we were very glad when she met Brian."

He leaned forward and lowered his voice. "He was a bigamist, you know, this Robert. Turned out he was already married. That's what it said in the paper."

Julie pursed her lips. She turned to Mrs Onslow. "So you can't think of anyone who would want to harm your daughter? You see, we think the killer may have known her."

Mrs Onslow's voice became shrill. "You mean someone from the hotel? Someone angry about the seal watching? Someone upset with what Emma predicted at a séance? That's the most ridiculous thing I ever heard! Could you please explain to me how any of that justifies murder, Detective?"

* * *

"Jennifer Draper. 3 St Nicholas Close, Friary Road, Glaveny," she gave her address for the record.

Neil checked that the machine was recording. They were sitting in a small makeshift interview room at the police station in Wells-next-the-Sea. A pile of cardboard boxes next to the desk meant there was barely enough room for the three of them.

Jen flicked her head. She was wearing a dark jumper and jeans tucked into a long pair of boots. "How can I help you, gentlemen?"

"Thanks for coming in on your day off," began Clayton. "We've been hearing that Emma Dawson thought she had psychic, uh, abilities."

The slightest flicker of an eyelid.

"Could you tell us about your sessions?"

She stared at Clayton. "Nothing to tell, really. Don't remember much about them." They waited. "What do you want to know?"

"Who was present at the séances?"

She hesitated. "I don't want to get anyone into trouble."

Clayton spoke slowly. "I'll remind you, Ms Draper, that we're investigating a murder here. Two in fact, and they may be linked. So anything you can do to help us would be most appreciated."

The barmaid blinked but said nothing.

Neil could see where this was heading and put on an encouraging smile. "You've already been extremely helpful. We've been talking to other people about the Frenchman you saw with Ms Dawson. But if she was holding séances in the village it might provide another line of inquiry, that's all."

She scowled. "I told you, I can't remember much about them. Sometimes we went round to Emma's with customers from the pub."

Clayton decided against pressing for names at this point. "And how long have you known Ms Dawson?"

"Years. Like I told you, we were at school together. Then we still saw quite a bit of each other when she was in Norwich, although less so after she got married and had the baby. We picked up again when she came back here."

"We hear that apparently she was able to communicate with Mother Julian. Or at least she said she could," said Clayton.

"Yes, that she did, after she came back from Norwich. She was in contact with her, definitely."

"How do you know?"

"Well, at these meetings, at the beginning, it was Mother Julian speaking. It wasn't Emma's normal voice. Deeper, somehow."

"Was it genuine?"

"Oh yes. She had us hold hands and all. She switched out the lights and had a candle in a kind of hollow skull that she put on the table, in the middle. She said it helped the spirits get in touch when we were all concentrating together."

"And what happened at these séances?"

"Well, sometimes she predicted like something that would happen. You know Len the painter?"

"He's one of the pub customers, right? Len Maitland?" He was on their list.

"Yes, Emma said at one of our sessions that something bad would happen to Len. Two days later, he fell off his ladder and broke a leg. He walks with a limp now because they didn't fix it right. He was proper scared after that because Emma predicted it."

"Was there anything else you can recall? Was Ms Dawson doing drugs?"

She looked outraged at the suggestion. "Drugs? Emma? Never!"

Neil was listening with his head resting on his hands. "Ms Draper, you say that these séances took place after you finished work at the pub." She nodded, "and that the people who accompanied you had been drinking there."

She brushed a strand of hair from her face. "So is it possible that they'd all had a bit too much to drink? Just because a painter falls off a ladder doesn't mean that Emma was psychic."

"You can believe me or not, but I'm telling you what I saw with my own two eyes. That girl had supernatural powers. Definitely."

Clayton stepped in. "All right. And do you know whether Emma had a séance in the days before she died?"

"I don't know. Sorry. The last time I was there was about three weeks ago." She looked at her watch. "Look, do you have many more questions? I've got a bus back to Glaveny in a few minutes."

"Just tell us what happened at the last séance, and you can still catch it," said Clayton.

Jen Draper frowned. "A teacher from Eddie's school was there with her husband at one session."

"Was Eddie ever there?" Clayton asked.

"No. He was in bed."

"Go on. What happened with the teacher?"

Jen Draper said Emma had been troubled because the connection with Mother Julian hadn't been working. "She got quite upset, actually. She was crying. She broke the circle and was wringing her hands like she was possessed."

"Was she in some kind of trance?"

"She was always in a trance, but this time you could see she was in conflict. I got scared and in the end the other two left. We had a cup of tea to calm Emma down."

"Is it possible that this was the last séance she had before she died?"

"Maybe. I don't know."

They were all silent.

Had Emma foreseen her own death?

Chapter 10

Inspector Stéphane Gallois stepped out of the shower and shaved carefully to avoid nicking the ends of his moustache. The local radio station was reporting on the search for a man suspected of murdering a British woman and he was trying not to smile.

It was the first time that the St Valéry *gendarmerie* had received a European arrest warrant for a murder. He pulled on his pale blue uniform polo shirt, stretching his neck to study himself in the mirror. He turned his face to the left and right to make sure the moustache was neatly trimmed and that his sideburns stopped halfway down his ears, just like the regulations said.

It was usually the municipal police who had to deal with foreigners. They tended to get a little boisterous after too many beers on the quayside, and got into the occasional brawl. Another branch of the *gendarmerie* dealt with the car crashes. Of course, Gallois' team had investigated murders before, but they were mostly domestics. This would make a change from organised crime and drug trafficking. A murder suspect wanted by the English was exciting.

"My tailor is rich," he said, with a broad smile into the bathroom mirror, spreading his lips wide to say "*reach*." He was looking forward to practising his English.

Gallois and a colleague had turned up at the suspect's bedsit at two in the afternoon on the previous day. Gilbert Dumont, a sergeant close to retirement, had seen it all, but like Gallois had never been part of a manhunt. After the press leak that morning, they were worried that their quarry had fled. And they were right. The flimsy door of Billard's garret on Quai du Romerel had yielded in seconds. A copy of the *Courrier Picard* lay on the table, headlines screaming.

"Looks like he left in a hurry," said Dumont.

Gallois rang the office.

A downstairs neighbour said he'd heard the door slamming a couple of hours earlier.

"He's not going far," Gallois said to his colleague. "Next time he switches his phone on, we'll get him."

The investigators spent the rest of the day combing through Billard's belongings. Of particular interest were a pair of hiking boots and some gumboots. They checked the size — forty-three. Corresponding to the British size nine mentioned by the UK authorities.

They'd trawled through the suspect's personal records. The job centre said he'd done a series of casual jobs, working as a cook at McDonalds and helping out at the campsite. But nobody had seen him in weeks.

His profile was pretty typical of the average thirty-one-year-old resident of St Valéry, Gallois thought. If he wasn't a fisherman, he'd probably only been able to get seasonal work in a place like this with such high unemployment.

This morning they were going to drive out to the spit in case any of his friends were seal watching.

Gallois went downstairs, where his wife Elise was washing the breakfast dishes before taking their two young children to school. He poured himself a bowlful of coffee, dropping a sugar cube into the dark liquid. He never ate anything in the morning. He drained the bowl in a couple of slurps.

Elise shook her head. She was fussing with the children. "We're on our way out. Running late."

"See you tonight," he said, kissing her on the lips as though he hadn't noticed her curtness.

She turned away, saying, "You stink of coffee."

He shrugged and bent down to kiss the boys. He was drinking his second coffee and scanning the front page of the paper when Dumont knocked on the front door a few minutes later.

"Let's go."

Gallois had always enjoyed the half-hour drive to the Plage du Hourdel when he took the kids to see the seals. "Doesn't really feel like work, does it?"

But today the air was cold. The seal pups had been born a couple of months ago so they might be lucky and find one of the volunteer watchers. They pulled up in front of a poster warning visitors not to get closer than 300 metres to the seals.

"There's a couple of them over there," said Dumont. He pointed to two men, wearing the blue jackets of the seal protection association, staring at the estuary. One was holding a large pair of binoculars, while the other was bent over a camera on a tripod.

They trudged slowly over the pebbles, pulling up their jacket collars against the northerly wind. The salt marshes stretched as far as the eye could see on the other side of the estuary. In front of them everything was grey — the shingle, the bay, the sky.

Hearing the crunch of shoes, one of the men turned round.

"See anything?" said Gallois.

The man stretched out his arm. Following it, they could make out two black heads bobbing in the water.

The detectives nodded. "*Adjudant-chef* Stéphane Gallois. We're looking for Michel Billard. Know him?" Dumont took out his notebook.

The seal spotters knew Billard, but only slightly. They suggested that Jean-Pierre Rossignol would be better able to help.

"But he'll be working today. He's a carpenter, isn't he?" the other said.

The two detectives took down their phone numbers and walked back to the car with the wind at their backs. As Dumont radioed the office, Gallois turned to him and winked.

Chapter 11

The wind was chasing a plastic bag across the car park by the Point Hotel when Julie returned to Glaveny with some witness appeals.

The constabulary had placed them in the local newspapers and on the police website. The flyer had a recent photograph of Emma, donated by her parents. It requested anyone who might have seen anything of interest to the murder case to contact the police. You never knew with these appeals, Julie thought. She'd been in Ipswich during the investigation into the murders of sex workers. The police had been inundated with responses from the public. In her experience, they were mostly useless, but sometimes a pattern emerged which could give a real boost to an investigation.

They needed it. They were still waiting to hear back from the French police, and nothing suspicious had been found among Emma Dawson's phone messages and voicemails. Julie stood in front of the Point Hotel and looked towards the saltmarsh.

Its desolate wastes stretched as far as the eye could see. She got back in the car and drove on to Pelham-next-the-Marsh. She left the flyers in shops along the High

Street and stopped at the pottery where she chatted for a while with the owner. They'd discovered during an earlier conversation that their sons were the same age. Julie was just leaving when she caught sight of an elderly man, leaning heavily on a walking stick, about to disappear inside a low flint cottage. She knew this was the home of the man they called the 'hermit of Pelham.' The smoke-stained curtains were pulled tightly shut.

On impulse, she followed him and reached the door just as he was turning to close it. She noticed immediately the eyepatch over his right eye. He was unshaven, and his cheeks were gaunt, and yellow as parchment. His shabby clothes hung in folds on his thin frame. The trousers appeared to be held up with string.

"Excuse me, sir . . ." Julie began. The door slammed in her face.

She shouted through the letterbox. "Police! Excuse me, sir, would you please open the door?" Not a sound came from inside.

She pushed the witness appeal through the letterbox and left it at that. Clayton had told her there was no point in questioning him. She checked her watch. She had to get to Wells-next-the-Sea to meet Neil at the station. Then she heard a loud barking coming from behind the cottage. She walked round to the side gate, and peered through its tall wooden slats. In the small backyard a huge black dog was outside the back door, howling, trotting backwards and forwards. Was it trying to get inside? She stepped back onto a twig which broke with a faint crack. The dog suddenly turned and lunged towards her, snarling. She was startled by the size of its jaws. But it was yanked back by its chain, rising onto its hind legs. Thank God for that chain, she thought, and hurried to the car.

* * *

Len Maitland, a thin man with a hook nose, shuffled into the interview room. He had a slight limp and walked with the aid of a cane. His moth-eaten jumper was slightly stained with remnants of food, his jeans smudged with traces of white paint. He arranged himself on a chair, one leg sticking straight out in front of him.

Julie began. "Tell us about the séances at Emma's place. Do you believe she had some kind of special powers?"

Len patted his leg. "Too right she did. Did you hear what happened to me? I only went once, and that was enough."

Julie leaned forward over the desk. "We did, but tell us in your own words."

Neil kept an eye on the tape recorder.

"Who was there that night?"

"Me and Jen were there. One of them from Oak Farm was there."

"Do you have the name?"

"He didn't say much. What was his name now? I'm afraid you'll have to ask his boss, I've clean forgot."

It must be one of the farmhands they'd spoken to after Jimmy's murder.

"Could you describe him?"

"Fair-haired young guy, about thirty I suppose. Been on the farm for a couple of years now. Does the vegetables. And I've see him at the pub too, with his mates. And with Emma." He paused.

Julie nodded. "So there we are at Emma's place . . ."

"Does she switch the lights off?" Neil asked.

Maitland cleared his throat and his forehead creased. "She switched off the main light, but she put this other light on a small table in front of us. So it weren't dark, no. It was weird though. It was like a skull. Then she had us all hold hands, sitting in a circle."

"What, on the floor?" Julie remembered the size of Emma's living room.

"She had a few plastic chairs. Emma was in an armchair. I had my arms stretched out with her on one side and the farmhand on the other. Jason! That's his name. And Jen was there too. She had the other armchair."

"Go on."

"So then Emma starts moaning and saying, 'Mother are you there?' I thought she meant her own mum, but I found out afterwards she meant Mother Julian. Then she looks at me, or rather she looked in my direction but she wasn't looking at me, she kind of looked through me. And then her voice changed, and she started moving her head from side to side. It was like she was struggling to understand something. Then she said, 'Oh no!' or something like that in a funny voice. And then straight after that she told me there would be an accident."

"An accident? Did she say it would happen to you specifically?"

"Not so I recall, no. But she looked at me when she spoke. Two days later I fell off my ladder when I was painting the King's Arms at Branstable, and now look at me." He gestured at his leg. "I might have died."

"Is it possible that you'd been so frightened by what she'd said, that you were nervous, which might have contributed to the accident?" Julie said.

Neil stifled a sigh. He clearly thought the supernatural angle was a load of mumbo-jumbo.

"Frightened? Me? I didn't think anything of it at the time. But after it happened, that's when I got really scared. She had supernatural powers, that one."

"And can you think of anyone else who might have had a similar experience? Someone who might bear her a grudge? Did you, for example?"

Maitland shook his head and began to massage his thigh. "It weren't her fault. If there's anyone to blame, I reckon it's Mother Julian."

"Who were the regulars at these séances, please, Mr Maitland?" Julie said.

"How should I know? I only went the once, I told you. Jen though. She'd know about the others."

“Ms Draper, the barmaid?” Neil said.

The painter nodded.

Julie and Neil exchanged a look. Why had the barmaid not mentioned the regulars? What did she have to hide?

Chapter 12

The sound of an electric saw filled the Rue des Moulins. The front door of Jean-Pierre Rossignol's workshop yawned open.

Rossignol, his hair pulled back into a ponytail, was standing in a pile of sawdust. He took off his protective mask when he noticed Gallois and Dumont.

"Michel Billard? The last time I saw him was a few days ago. He'd been to England." Their association had plans to map the seals' movements by tagging them. He drew an imaginary map in the air with one finger. "They go like this, along the coast you see, across the Channel and round to Norfolk. And to other places as well, of course. But that's how we found out about Glaveny. The *entente cordiale* of seals. Maybe they're related to each other."

"How well do you know Monsieur Billard?"

"Very well. I've known him for years. He wouldn't harm a fly, I'm telling you."

"They all say that."

Rossignol added, "There was that thing with his ex-wife, but they never proved anything."

"What thing?" said Gallois.

"She committed suicide about three years ago in Rouen. He was accused of murdering her, but nobody believed it. The court dismissed the case."

"Relatives?"

"I don't know. He didn't talk about his parents. He didn't have a girlfriend." He picked up his saw. "Sorry, I can't help."

"Get in touch if you hear from him," said Gallois. As they were leaving, he turned back, and said, "I'd remind you that it's a criminal offence to do anything to help a murder suspect. You'd be an accomplice to a crime."

When they'd gone Rossignol put down his saw and went straight into the kitchen to find his phone. He texted Billard: *Cops on your trail. You OK?*

Then he hesitated before pressing Send. He knew that calls and texts could be traced and monitored. He deleted the message and went to the front door. He looked down the steep hill lined with fishermen's cottages painted in shades of blue and pink that looked incongruous at this time of year. The police were out of sight.

How could he get hold of Billard to warn him? He remembered that his friend had said he'd contact him. All he could do now was wait. The last thing he wanted was to put his friend in danger. Maybe he'd already said too much. But what if he *had* committed a murder? Killed that girl in England? Rossignol picked up the white mask and went back to work.

* * *

Billard's enforced camping experience was wearing him out. With all the campsite facilities closed, he had only the icy waters of a nearby stream to wash in and it almost took his breath away. For the rest of the time, he kept the tent zipped up and sat shivering inside its flimsy shelter. Why hadn't he brought his sleeping bag? The mere sound of the wind rattling the privet hedge was enough to unnerve him. His senses were alive to every twig breaking.

Once, in the middle of the night, he scrambled to his knees after hearing the hoot of a screech owl. It sounded unnervingly human.

One morning, he heard a dog sniffing at the entrance to the tent, followed by a steady stream as it urinated on it. He prayed that it didn't have an owner, but heard no one. He froze at every sound. Something crashed over the hedge and landed with a thump beside the tent. He sat trembling and by the time he'd summoned the courage to pull the zip down slightly to peer through the hole, he could see the tell-tale white scut of a buck deer disappearing behind a caravan.

How much longer could he stand this? He spent hours debating whether to hand himself in. Without a newspaper, he didn't even know if the cops were still on his trail.

As dusk fell he went foraging for supplies in the dustbins behind Lidl. He slept fitfully, dreaming about food — a crusty baguette, its moist centre bearing no relation to the soggy stick he'd pulled out of the bin. In a recurring nightmare, he sliced into a creamy Camembert, but as he was about to pick it up he saw that the cheese was running with blood.

After an entire day spent listening to the rain falling on the tent, he'd had enough. As soon as it stopped, he unzipped the tent, turning to make sure he'd left nothing behind. The pungent smell of stale food and sweat followed him out. So what if they found the tent in this lonely corner of the campsite, in any case, it wouldn't reopen until next April. He climbed over the gate and in the moonlight, it took him about an hour to hike back into town across fields and through woods. He moved furtively, keeping to the shadows. As he made his way up the Rue des Moulins towards Rossignol's house, he noticed the carpenter's bicycle leaning against the wall. He was comforted to see that the light was on. Too afraid to use his phone, he tapped on the door. A curtain twitched and then his friend opened the door.

"What the fuck are you doing? I've had the police here, looking for you. I told them I hadn't seen you in days. What if they're watching me? Your picture's been on TV."

"I need help. I'm going crazy, I've not spoken to a soul for days." He saw Rossignol's gaze fall on his grubby clothes, the shoes covered in mud. He hadn't shaved since he'd left the bedsit.

"What do you need? Have a shower and a shave while you're here. Use my stuff but for Christ's sake be quick about it."

Billard was already taking his clothes off as he went into the bathroom.

He came back into the workshop, smelling of Rossignol's aftershave.

"Look, you've got to hand yourself in," said Rossignol.

"I can't. What do you think they'd do to me?"

"But how are you going to survive? Where have you been all this time?"

Billard said nothing. He couldn't tell him. He fingered the knife in his pocket. "I just need some cash to keep me going. You've got to help me."

Rossignol hesitated, "Look at you. What are you getting to eat?"

"Never mind. I just need a few euros. Whatever you can." Billard's hand tightened on the Laguiole.

Rossignol fished in his pocket and took out a twenty euro bill. He held out the blue note to Billard. "Here, take this. But don't come back again."

"Thanks." Billard stuffed the note into his jeans and walked out of the house. Straight into the arms of two waiting policemen.

Chapter 13

"The lad's been drawing? What kind of drawing?" Clayton held the phone to his ear and doodled a daisy shape on a notepad as he listened.

A couple of minutes later he found Julie and Neil at the coffee machine. "I've just had a call from Dawson. He says Eddie's been drawing pictures, and that it might be of interest to us."

Julie dropped her cup into the rubbish bin. "Is he talking again?"

"No. But Dawson'll drop off one or two pictures to see if they make any sense to us."

"Maybe the kid's got second sight as well," Neil said. "Though if the mother had second sight, how come she didn't predict her own death?"

"Maybe she did," said Clayton. "But maybe she didn't have time to call Ghostbusters."

* * *

It was after five when reception called to say that Brian Dawson was downstairs. Clayton and Julie took him to an interview room.

"How's Eddie?" Julie asked.

"Hard to tell. He's a closed book. He always has been quiet with me," Dawson said. "But now it's like he's struck dumb with grief. He never says a thing."

"Bed-wetting? Nightmares?"

Dawson nodded, adding, "Poor kid."

"Where is he now?"

"At home with my girlfriend and her daughter."

"Does he confide in them? In the girl?" Julie asked.

Dawson shook his head. "Lauren's a bit older. I suppose they've not got much in common." He opened a plastic bag and took out two thick sheets of paper which he unrolled and placed on the table. "I've brought these. Eddie's new school in Norwich has arranged art therapy for him, in the hope that it would help him come to terms with losing his mother. At first he didn't draw anything special. Just black loops. But recently the pictures are much more detailed, and I was wondering if he's trying to tell us something. I thought it might be of some help."

They stood and looked at the first drawing. The upper half of the sheet was crayoned in blue, and the bottom half green. The sky and the marsh. A stick figure was drawn in pencil in the foreground. It had its arm forwards as though striking something. At its feet lay a long white smudge. Was it supposed to be human? Swirls of white chalk completed the picture, partly covering the scene.

The chalk must be mist, Clayton thought. But what was the smudge? A body? "Let's look at the other one," he said.

It was more detailed. The child had drawn seal shapes, and what could have been ducks, or seagulls, walking in the mud. Two stick figures were in the foreground, the taller one wearing a skirt which had been filled in with pencil. But this time, in the background, there were two shapes, one human and the other on four legs. Its limbs were splayed and its hair stood on end, like a cartoon cat with its tail sticking up.

"Two people. A mother and child? A parent and child? Is this Eddie and Emma? And why a child? Or is this stick figure in the background Eddie?" Clayton stabbed the picture with his finger as he went from one character to another.

"That figure at the back, it's not a woman with the child. He puts long hair on the woman in front. Look," Julie said.

Clayton turned to Dawson. "And Eddie's never given you any explanation for these?"

"No. I hope you don't think I'm wasting your time."

"Not at all. And we'd be grateful for any others that might look interesting. May we photocopy them?"

Dawson was escorted to the lift.

"This is doing my head in," Clayton said.

They showed the drawings to Neil, who merely said, "Well, he's not Picasso, that's for sure."

Julie scrutinised the second painting again. "I can't help thinking the child is trying to tell us something," she said.

Chapter 14

"They've got our man!" Bligh burst into the office.

Clayton put down his half-eaten bacon sandwich and swallowed. "The French guy? Great!"

Bligh adjusted her spectacles. "Right, so let's get a press conference sorted. The DNA is a match. His boots are the same size as the footprints at the crime scene, and he had a history of domestic violence." She might as well have said, 'case closed.'

"Actually, we're making some progress on another front, ma'am. There might be a link to the Jimmy Spratley murder — we're getting some info from the kid . . ."

But Bligh wasn't listening. Clayton hated the way she always seemed to think she was two steps ahead of everyone else.

"And after that, get your things. You're going to France," she added. "Take Neil or Julie with you."

"Yes, ma'am." Clayton stood up and studied the map behind him. Glaveny Point stretched out like a lobster claw. The macabre triangle of death was marked by pin tacks, its northern tip on the Pelham marshes where the blackened and gnawed remains of Jimmy Spratley's heart had been found. Then the village to the south where he'd been dumped in the churchyard. And a couple of miles west of that, the boat at Branstable Quay, where Emma's body had been discovered.

Forensics said she'd been murdered the day before she was found. The 1 spot with barbed-wire fencing was a meadow on the marsh where cows grazed near the Pelham windmill. The killer must have dragged the body into a car, then waited until dark before taking it to the boat.

Clayton went to find Julie. "How's your French?"

"Did they get him?" she replied.

"Yes. I want you to come with me to interview him."

But instead of looking pleased at the opportunity to travel abroad, she frowned and reached for her handbag. "Let me make a phone call."

"Child care?"

She scowled at him.

* * *

It was a long and complicated journey from Norwich to St Valéry-sur-Somme, which gave them plenty of time to talk. Despite working on the same team for more than a year, Clayton realised that they hardly knew each other. He was closer to Neil in a male-bonding kind of way.

"It's not that I didn't want to come on this trip." She swayed gently in her seat as the Eurostar sped through the Kent countryside on the way to Lille. She was folding and unfolding a paper napkin. "Thanks for asking me."

"Family stuff, I presume." Clayton really didn't want to encourage Julie to pour out her troubles to him. He looked out of the window.

"No, I want to tell you. It's not a secret. It's just that I don't generally talk about my private life."

He grinned. "Don't tell me you're having an affair with Nuclear Winter?" This was the police commissioner's nickname.

Julie didn't laugh. "I was just going to tell you that I'm a single mum, and it makes my life a bit complicated. That's all. But it doesn't affect how I do my job."

"It's okay, Julie. Nobody's suggesting otherwise." He watched her relax into her seat. "Boy or girl?"

"Boy. He's six."

"What's he called?"

"Oliver — Ollie." She showed him the photo of a curly-haired child on the screen of her phone.

Clayton smiled. "He's a cute little lad."

"Same age as Eddie, isn't he? The first time I saw Eddie, I wanted to give him a cuddle, he seemed so vulnerable. Poor thing. Have you got kids?"

"No I'm separated from my wife."

"That's tough."

"Yeah. She didn't want to move to Norwich. I thought it might be a fresh start, but it didn't work out that way."

He looked out the window as sheep grazing in fields flashed by. Should he tell her the rest of it? How Claire had deserted him for a doctor at the hospital? He decided not to. He didn't want the entire office to know about his humiliation. He sat back and closed his eyes.

Julie had been in the force for ten years now. Clayton hoped she wouldn't broach the issue of promotion. She must know it wasn't up to him, yet he always had the feeling that she was nipping at his heels. Why did women treat him like this? Somehow they always found a way to dominate him.

It had probably started with his mother. She'd ruled the household. Clayton and his dad got it in the neck every time they forgot to take off their shoes when they came in. His sister Melanie, on the other hand, could do no wrong. He remembered the lies she told their mother about his behaviour, about how he'd been caught smoking in the school toilets, how he'd been in a bust-up in the playground. It had all been made up.

He must have been ten and Melanie eight when she'd accused him of giving him a Chinese burn. She showed their mother her sore red arm. Clayton knew she'd done it to herself just to get him into trouble. He'd really felt like hitting her then. His father never got involved. He would hide behind the newspaper. Clayton knew he'd get nowhere by calling his sister a liar. Instead, he went into the back garden and took his frustrations out on the dustbin. Or he ran upstairs and slammed his bedroom door so hard that it shook on its hinges. He hadn't seen Melanie in years.

Julie interrupted his thoughts. "So what do you think about Winter, anyway?"

He grinned at this. "Don't get me started! Waste of taxpayers' money if you ask me. They could get rid of them all, as far as I'm concerned."

"What about Bligh? Do you rate her?"

Clayton hesitated. He usually didn't gossip with colleagues, particularly with the women. That said, he'd always wondered whether the boss was a bit insecure, and that's what made her so assertive. On the other hand, he thought, it must be tough for a woman, the nick was still a male-dominated environment.

"Yes. She's dead good," he said. "Tough cookie." He added, " I don't envy her that job. Lots of stress and uncertainty at the moment. The force has got to find twenty million quid in savings over the next three years. At least you and I only have to worry about our cases. She's got all the paperwork and a whole lot of other shit." He leaned back in his seat. "This is the most troubling case I've seen yet."

"Me too," Julie said. "Though you had that serial killer in Blackpool before you moved to Norwich, didn't you?"

He nodded. "Aye, Ringo."

She raised her eyebrows.

"We called him that because he was from Liverpool. And because he collected the rings of his victims. We only got him because he over-reached himself."

"Wasn't he pawning the rings?"

"Yes, it was a pawnbroker who tipped us off. I think that at the end he wanted to be caught. But this is different. And of course with a kid involved, the media interest is huge."

"I was in Ipswich for the Suffolk Strangler. You should have seen the number of journalists who turned up for that one. They came from all over the world. And of course they all started behaving like amateur sleuths."

"That must have been fun," said Clayton.

"Bloody circus. But the DNA got him in the end, thank God." Julie looked out of the window for a while, then took out a detective novel and read. Clayton glanced over at her from time to time, but she never looked up from her book.

The sun was setting as they reached St Valéry. They raced in their hired car across the salt marsh towards the town.

"This is stunning! Can you pull over?" Julie got out her phone and wound down the window to take a picture of the orange-tinted clouds. "Wow! Look at the horizon, it's vast!"

The painted houses of St Valéry ran in a line along the quay. They followed signs to their hotel. Its wooden turrets looked out over the estuary.

"Weird, isn't it?" Clayton said, picking up a leaflet about seal viewing while the receptionist checked them into their rooms. "It's like Glaveny, only French."

* * *

Clayton ran through the messages on his phone, joined Julie in the lobby and they set off for the *gendarmerie.* Stéphane Gallois came out to greet them, speaking in proficient English. Clayton's French ran out after "*bonjour*" and "*merci*" and he'd relied on Julie since they arrived in France.

"Thank you for coming so quickly," said Gallois. "We arrested Billard on suspicion of murder, but we can only hold him for another twenty-four hours before we have to present him before a judge or let him go."

He took them into an empty office where he got out a file and flicked through some papers. "The DNA is a match," he said.

Clayton nodded. "And the boot size too."

"Of course we intend to ask the judge to place him under formal investigation."

"That's the equivalent of charging him," Julie explained.

"It doesn't always lead to a formal charge though," said Gallois. "Nowadays in France we are more like you, innocent until proved guilty."

He led the way down a dark corridor to a small interrogation room, opening a side door so that Julie could watch from behind a screen.

The suspect was sitting at the table, looking at his hands. His whole body was taut. A woman lawyer was next to him. He glanced up when he heard the approaching steps.

Clayton introduced himself and sat at the table with Gallois. He made sure it was okay to speak in English.

"You understand me, right?"

"Yes, monsieur."

The lawyer intervened. "I wish to have an interpreter present. Given the seriousness of the charges pending against my client, I think it's essential."

Gallois sighed. He stood up and told Clayton that this would take a while to sort out.

"Do you want to do this tomorrow?" Clayton asked.

"No, just give us a few minutes. You can wait in my office."

Gallois came to collect them about half an hour later. It was eight thirty and Clayton's stomach was rumbling. His dream of steak and chips in a quayside café was fading fast.

This time, a young woman sat next to Billard at the table, with the lawyer on his other side. Gallois and Clayton faced them.

"Mr Billard, you are aware that some serious charges are being laid against you? We need you to help us understand what happened. What were you doing in Glaveny?"

"Monsieur, I already told the police here. I was in Glaveny for a week to speak to people about seals. My association here can tell you that. I spoke with the fishermen, the wardens, the boatman, that's all."

"But you met people at the pub. You had intimate relations with Emma Dawson."

"That's not a crime," said the lawyer in English.

Clayton continued, addressing Billard. "Emma Dawson was killed while you were in Glaveny. We need to know your movements between the Saturday afternoon and the Sunday when her body was found."

"I didn't do it!" he said. The lawyer touched his arm with fingernails painted a bright violet.

"On the Sunday morning I was writing up my notes at the bed and breakfast. I can't remember what time I left, but I think it was in the late morning. I needed to catch the train from Norwich at one o'clock. I think I still have the receipt." He looked defiantly at Clayton.

"And what about the Saturday? Where were you then? On the marsh?" Clayton leaned forward.

Billard scratched his head. "Yes, I was on the marsh. In the afternoon it was misty."

"Exactly. And where were you when the mist came down?"

"I don't remember. I went walking along the Point, where the seals are. But I couldn't see very well because of the mist."

"Were you alone?"

"Yes, sir."

"Did you have a car to get around Glaveny?"

"I walked. A couple in the pub gave me a lift one day, but that was on Thursday, I think, after we took a boat trip."

"What couple?"

"They were from London."

Gallois intervened. "Maybe you could tell us about what happened to your ex-wife."

Billard stiffened and his fist closed on the table. The lawyer whispered something to him. He answered her, then said to Gallois, "She was a depressive. She was bipolar. And the case was dismissed."

The lawyer said something to Gallois which was translated as, "You can't dredge up an old case, which was unproven by the way, to try guilt by association. You cannot go down this route."

She and Gallois scowled at each other across the table. Gallois shut the file with a flourish and said, "We'll see what Madame le Juge says about that."

He and Clayton stepped outside the interview room, where they were joined by Julie.

"It's a bit of a coincidence, don't you think?" said Gallois. "A man who may have killed his ex-wife three years ago now suspected of murdering a girlfriend."

"But it was unproven, right?" Julie said.

Gallois smiled. "Not proved doesn't mean he didn't do it."

"And he resisted arrest after we put out the Europol alert," said Clayton. "But we've still got some unresolved issues."

"Oh?"

"The car, for example. We think Emma Dawson was killed on the marsh on the Saturday afternoon and then driven to the place where she was found the next day. If Billard didn't have a car, it's possible there was an accomplice. Or that the murderer was someone else altogether."

"What do you think the judge will decide?" Julie said.

Gallois shrugged. "I imagine she'll place him under formal investigation."

"We're going to have to extradite him, of course," said Clayton.

Gallois raised his eyebrows. "I'm afraid that won't be possible. France does not extradite its citizens for trial."

"You're kidding me, right?"

Gallois stroked his moustache and shook his head.

"If he has committed a murder and is arrested in France, he will be tried in France. Anyway, we look forward to collaborating with you."

Chapter 15

After they had put the children to bed, Neil dropped into his favourite armchair by the fireside and opened a bottle of red wine. He poured a glass for his wife, Megan. "This could be my chance. I've got a couple of days all on my own to wrap up the loose ends in the Glaveny case while the Lone Ranger and Tonto are away."

Megan sipped her wine. "You're a bit distracted by this case, aren't you?"

"It's horrible. Still, I'm just waiting for Sam to drop the ball so that I can pick it up. I think the DCI's got it in for him."

"It's certainly time you got a promotion. A little extra would help, wouldn't it?"

"You can say that again. Especially with Christmas around the corner." Neil had no idea how he was going to afford presents for his two teenagers with his previous two wives as well as gifts for his sons with Megan. It got harder every year.

"What about Julie? Is she still brown-nosing?"

"It's hard to know what Bligh thinks about her. They're both women, but very different. One's intuitive and the other's a hard-bitten professional. But hints are being dropped that one of us could be out on our ear."

Megan reached out to take her husband's stubby fingers and raised them to her lips. "Oh no! Why didn't you tell me?"

He patted her hand and took a long sip of his wine. "No point worrying till it happens, pet. But that's why we're all under pressure to get this case solved. And, like I say, now's my chance."

* * *

The next morning, Neil drove to work early, ran up the stairs to the office and leafed through the Glaveny case file. After about half an hour he'd worked out a plan.

Driving through drizzle, he went to Oak Farm outside Glaveny. Dogs began to bark as he pulled up in front of a large gabled house with a barn attached to it. He could see an outhouse across the courtyard and a couple of others at the entrance to a field.

The front door opened before he could knock. The farmer appeared, shouting to the dogs to be quiet. He was a big man, middle-aged, and wearing wellingtons. "Hello there. I was just on my way out."

"I need to talk to that farmhand of yours again — Jason," Neil said.

"He might be able to help with enquiries into the double murder in the village. The boy and the waitress."

The farmer pointed to one of the outhouses. Neil found a young man chopping wood. He was wearing a vest, and his discarded pullover lay on the floor. As he raised the axe Neil noticed his toned muscles. He wiped his muddy hands on his jeans and came forward to shake Neil's hand.

"I hear you went to the séances at Emma's place," Neil said.

Jason looked at him as though to say 'so what?' He put down the axe. His right arm was black with tattoos which tumbled down from his shoulder.

"I just need to know who was there apart from you."

"It depends. Usually three or four of us."

Neil waited. "So there was you, Emma, Jen the barmaid . . ."

"Yes that's right."

"Anyone else?"

"I can't remember."

Neil looked up from his notebook. Had everyone in this village been struck by amnesia?

"And what happened then?"

The farmhand sighed. "I don't recall much. The thing is, she put a spell on us. We all held hands around the table and she contacted Mother Julian. That much I can tell you. But as for the rest of it . . ." He shrugged. "Sorry."

He picked up the axe again and Neil turned to go.

Then as though remembering something, he said, "Oh, by the way, what's your shoe size?"

The axe came down and split a log neatly in half. Jason leaned on the handle and wiped his forehead. "Nine," he said.

As Neil walked back to the car he noticed some barbed-wire fencing holding back a flock of sheep. The top wire was missing and strands of sheep wool fluttered from the next line down. He took a closer look. There was a distance of about two yards between the fence posts. He headed back to the outhouse.

This time, Neil was less friendly. "Know anything about the missing barbed wire on the fence here?"

Jason looked puzzled. "Missing wire?"

Neil pointed towards the fence.

"Sorry. No idea. I've not been asked to fix it. Better ask my boss."

"Don't worry, I will. Now, about these séances. You say Emma Dawson put a *spell* on you all. What happened then?"

Jason lifted the axe, seemed to weigh it, then lowered it again. He looked into the gloom. "She must have done. She said Mother Julian wanted to test us. I only realised what had happened to me after I woke up having slit the throat of one of the farm tabbies. I don't know why I did it, but that's the only thing I can think of."

"And where did you put it?"

"In a bin in the village. I had blood all over my hands. That's when I came to my senses."

"And did you go back to a séance after that?"

"Yes. I told you, she had a power over us. And we had this kind of pact."

"And none of you thought that she might be practising hypnosis without a licence?"

The farmhand shook his head. "Didn't know you needed a licence."

Neil looked at Jason's wrist. "And when you say you had a pact, you mean you were all members of a kind of sect? Do you all have that daisy tattoo?"

Jason's left hand covered his wrist. "Nothing wrong with that."

"But that's how you identify the group, right?"

The hand fell away. "Yes."

Chapter 16

The riverside bench was the most private place Clayton could find. He could feel its frozen slats through his trousers. His scarf protected him from the full force of the blistering wind, but he couldn't escape the shrill blast down the phone. He'd just told Bligh that the French wouldn't extradite their suspect.

"What do you mean they don't extradite their nationals? We'll see about that!"

"Even if they did, it would take months, even years to get him to Norwich," he said. "His lawyer would definitely contest it."

None of this satisfied his boss. "But they've charged the suspect now, right? We can announce that at least?"

"Yes, ma'am. Last night, after we left. Billard didn't get bail. We're going to have a coffee with the chief investigator now, and then we'll be on our way back." He rang off.

He wandered into the hotel car park, where Julie was talking to Gallois.

Clayton greeted them in his bad French. "As I suspected, HQ is none too pleased about this extradition issue."

Gallois shrugged. "This doesn't happen very often, of course. I can remember only one case, a few years ago, a murder in Birmingham I think. The trial was held in France and the killer got thirty years. But it was a long time before the trial was held."

Clayton was balling his hands inside his pockets. "That's very helpful."

They walked towards the main square. As they passed a high brick building on the left, Gallois pointed to the locked gate and said, "That used to be our office, it's the old *gendarmerie*. Private apartments now. Lovely view." They peered into the courtyard.

"And that's where the suspect was staying." Gallois pointed to a shabby three-storey building on the other side of the street.

"Opposite the *gendarmerie*! Fancy that!" Julie said.

They reached a café whose outdoor terrace was protected from the cold with transparent plastic drapes and overhead heaters. Gallois took out an e-cigarette.

Stylish, thought Clayton. "What else are you working on at the moment?"

"Trafficking, people smuggling, illegal immigrants."

"I thought they were all in Calais."

"I think in Calais they are mainly from Africa — you know, Sudan and Eritrea. The ones who come here are from Eastern Europe. There are a lot of Ukrainians. They come along the coast from Belgium."

"And then where do they go?"

"Sometimes we catch them. We are helped by the seal monitors and the birdwatchers who are in the saltmarshes and on the estuary with their binoculars. Then we send them home. "

"Do they want to stay here?"

"Of course not. They all want to go to England. They speak English. They think your country is better. It's El Dorado!"

Clayton grunted. "Yeah, well." They sipped their coffees. "We have illegal migrants round us too. They do seasonal work on the farms. And I think they're mostly Ukrainians. From time to time we bust them. They're good workers. But we also have the travellers, the Roma."

"Les Roms! They beg on the streets. They steal from tourists. That's a big problem here. The government is doing nothing about it. And if we arrest them, they start thieving again as soon as they get out."

"Tell us about it," Julie said. "The Roma beggars and pickpockets are a huge problem for us in Norwich. But it's like the migrant issue, the problem is finding the Mr Big who's making money from them."

Gallois sat back on his wicker chair and exhaled a cloud of vapour. He looked at his watch and called for the bill.

"This is a lovely spot," Julie said. "It reminds me of Glaveny, with the seal colony too. It would be fun if St Valéry were twinned with Glaveny."

"We're already twinned with an English town: Battle. William of Normandy set off from here to invade England in 1066. There are plenty of historical plaques around the town about it."

Clayton paid and they got up to leave. They strolled across the square to the river, where the tide was high. As if on cue, a seal's shiny head bobbed up in the current.

Chapter 17

His knock was firm but polite. Not a sound came from inside the flint cottage in Pelham. But Neil noticed a line of smoke billowing from the chimney in the prevailing wind.

He knocked again, louder this time. Still nothing. He opened the letterbox and shouted, "Police! Open up."

He rubbed his hands together for warmth. After another minute, he heard a shuffling sound. The key turned in the lock, and the door opened. Neil resisted the temptation to push it open and walk inside.

The man who opened it was fully clothed, but in rags. Neil held up his warrant card. "Anglian CID, sir. Detective Sergeant Neil Pringle. May I come in?"

The old man stood aside to let him pass. He led Neil into a kitchen piled high with rubbish and newspapers. Two bony cats brushed past and escaped into a neighbouring room filled with the stench of cat piss. An aluminium bowl stood on the lino with some milk in it.

Neil wrinkled his nose. "Mr Hopking. We're investigating the murder of the waitress from the Point Hotel in Glaveny. We believe that you may be able to help us."

Hopking remained standing. On a rickety table an empty coffee cup stood on a plate full of crumbs. Two wooden chairs were pulled up beside it. Neil looked through the clutter to the kitchen window, and saw trees overhanging a pocket-sized back garden. A Great Dane was tugging on a chain attached to a ring on a moss-covered stone wall.

"What of it?" Hopking said. "Your colleague pushed a flyer through my door. I don't know why you think I can help. I never heard of that woman."

"When were you last on the marsh?"

"Can't remember. Most days I s'pose."

"Were you on the marsh on Saturday or Sunday, the weekend of November the first, with the dog?"

The man scratched his yellow-grey hair. "I told you, I go down the marsh most days. It's a free country." He spat the words through a missing front tooth.

"I just want to know if you saw something. Your dog may have unearthed something of interest to the investigation."

Hopking stared at him with his one good eye.

Neil couldn't tell whether he was getting through or not. "When you go walking on the marsh, do you let the dog off the leash?"

"Maybe I do, maybe I don't."

Outside, the huge black dog was pacing up and down. Neil could see its ribs. It looked like it was starving. He remembered the heart buried on the marsh.

Hopking followed his gaze. "I'm a victim too, you know. But the police were never interested in my problems. I'm not good enough for you lot."

"What happened?"

"I've had youths come round here throwing stones at Caesar over the fence. They've stoned him!" He was shaking with rage. "The last time, a rock hit him smack on the side. I could show you the scar. I telephoned the police in Wells and they didn't even send a bobby round! Same thing in Holt!"

"How recently was this? Did you know these boys?"

"How could I? It was dark. I just heard them laughing outside the house, a gang of them. The last time was only a few weeks ago."

Neil handed his card to Hopking. "I'll follow this up. And if you remember anything that you think might be of assistance in our murder inquiry, please call."

Neil left the house, checking his watch. He'd have time for a quick lunch in the village and maybe catch the barmaid at the end of her shift.

He arrived just as Jen Draper was leaving the pub. "Busy day?"

"So-so."

Neil caught up with her. "Where's your tattoo, then, Ms Draper?" She said nothing. Maybe there was the faintest flush on her cheeks, but he couldn't be sure.

He continued. "We can call every villager into the station to find out whether they're a member of your club. It wouldn't take very long at all. I know all about the dead pets, by the way. And maybe one of your members is a murderer. So I suggest that you help me by telling me exactly who came along to those séances instead of playing pass the parcel again."

"I told you. You know about Len and the others."

Neil drew her over to one of the wooden trestle tables in front of the pub, and they sat down in a timid ray of sunlight. The seats were still damp. "So let's go through this again."

"What do you want to know?"

"Names. All of them. The regulars. The *members*." He emphasised the last word.

"I can tell you who was there, but like I said the last time, I can't remember what happened exactly."

"Except that you were hypnotised by Emma Dawson."

"Yes, that's true. But only the one who was told knew what Mother Julian wanted them to do."

"And what were you asked to do?"

"Emma said we had to sin to be forgiven. I was told to dig a grave in the churchyard. But I swear I didn't know what it was for. It wasn't me that killed that child! I only knew I'd done it after I put the spade away in the shed at home."

"That's what we call an accessory to murder, Ms Draper."

Her eyes were wide open. She pulled her jacket tighter around her.

"And the tattoo?"

Jen bent and pulled up the hem of her jeans. The blue daisy was emblazoned on her ankle.

Neil's pulse raced. One of the group must have killed Jimmy Spratley, and possibly Emma herself. But even if the waitress was channelling Mother Julian from the other side, why would she want her medium dead?

"Names, please, Ms Draper."

"Well, like I say, there was Len the painter, then there was Becky from next door . . ."

Neil interrupted her. "Emma's neighbour? Becky Berry?"

She nodded. "Then Jason from Oak Farm. And Bob the warden. And one of the boatmen, but I can't remember his name. He only started coming recently."

He'll have a tattoo, thought Neil. That shouldn't be too hard. Now the warden was in the frame, along with a boatman.

"Anyone else?"

"I think that's it."

"As I said, we could bring in everyone from the village and check their tattoos."

She said nothing.

Neil scribbled in his notepad. "What about the Frenchman? Was he there?"

"No. At least, not when I was there."

Neil wondered why she and the farmhand hadn't stopped attending the séances, once they realised what they'd done.

Jen seemed to read his mind. "Why didn't I leave? Like I told you, Emma had this power over us. And we were part of this group, see?"

"You mean like a sect? With the tattoos?"

"That's right. Sometimes I wondered whether it was really Mother Julian communicating, or if it was Emma herself deciding what we had to do." She leaned towards him and reached out to touch his arm. "But you won't mention what I just told you, will you, Officer? You see, we were supposed to keep it secret."

"And what about the farmhand? Why did he keep coming back?"

"Well, Jason was her boyfriend, so he would, wouldn't he?"

Chapter 18

Clayton kicked off his flip-flops and stretched out his legs on the sofa.

He took a deep breath and tried to relax. A classical guitar CD was playing softly in the background. It was his first weekend off in the month since Jimmy Spratley's death. Would he take the car to the coast for a run, or just wander round to the gym? He turned to the window. It was a bright day, not too much wind.

He felt lonely. His loneliness was like a creature waiting in the corner of the living room, ready to pounce. It had been crouched there ever since Claire had left. He'd never felt lonely before. All of his pursuits since school had been solitary, and he'd been happy with his own company. The guitar, the running, put him into a kind of meditative state, the perfect antidote to the electronic devices demanding his attention. He even sought out solitude. Only in his job was he expected to be a team player.

Time and time again his temper got him into trouble. The pen-pushers had sent him on an anger management course before he and Claire had moved to Norwich. He'd told them he was just as harsh on himself as he was on his colleagues, but they still made him go. At least they didn't block his promotion. He'd lashed out during the Ringo investigation, after a witness went back on his statement. He'd gone to his desk and swept everything off it right in front of everyone. Unfortunately, the computer had gone with it.

He remembered pushing open the door to the weekend course in Manchester, feeling like someone on their way to a meeting of Alcoholics Anonymous. It was held in a nondescript office block next to the Palace Theatre, where *Mother Goose* was playing. Neither he nor the five other guys in the room had taken it seriously. All they had to do was show up.

A couple of them had already had time off for stress-related issues. Another had punched a colleague. He told Clayton he'd just got fed up with being called "Tess." His last name was Tickle.

After the session, Claire had started to tease him, saying, "Calm down, dear," all the time.

He went upstairs and decided against changing the sheets. They could wait another couple of weeks, surely? He threw a towel into the washing machine. That too could wait.

Then he went round the living room with the hoover, vacuuming up crumbs, and ignoring the tomato stains on the matching sofa. The hoover made an alarming whooshing noise that he hadn't noticed before. He put it back in the cupboard and decided to tackle the washing up piled high in the kitchen sink. He thrust his hand into the water and pulled out two sodden chunks of chicken tikka masala which were blocking the plughole.

At least I'm organised at work, he thought, as he gave the plates and cutlery a cursory wipe and put them away.

He picked up his guitar, set up his music stand and began flicking through some sheet music. He was dipping into a packet of crisps when his phone rang. He traced the sound to the kitchen table. A photo of Claire flashed up on the screen. Should he answer?

Keep cool, Clayton, he said to himself.

"So how's Norfolk's most famous detective?" she said.

"Am I? That's not how it feels from this angle. How are you? Lost your phone for a year?"

"I know. Sorry. I was just calling for a chat. I was reading about your case, and how you were in France catching a suspect. It all sounds terribly exciting."

"Glad you think so. But I was only there for a day. It took hours to get there, and we only just got back. How's work?" As soon as he'd asked, he wished he hadn't. It made him think of lover-boy.

"Oh, not too bad. The usual. NFN." Normal for Norfolk. Their private joke. He could picture her in her dark senior nurse's uniform.

"I was just thinking about you when you rang."

"Really? I often think about you too."

He hesitated. "Me too — often."

"How about meeting for a catch-up drink?" she said.

What could be the harm in that? "That would be nice. Let me see how the next few days pan out." What should he do? He didn't want to arrange a date immediately, he needed to think. "I'll text you when I've looked at my schedule."

"Look forward to seeing you, then." She rang off.

You fool, he said to himself.

* * *

On the Monday morning, Neil caught sight of Julie in the cafeteria.

"Seen the singing policeman yet?"

"Who? Sam? He's in. He wants to see us about Glaveny."

"Coming up in the Tardis?" Neil asked. They stepped into the lift together.

Neil pressed their floor number. "You worried about the cuts?"

"Why, should I be?"

He knew he'd rattled her. "I would be if I were from Suffolk." The doors opened and Julie pushed past him.

"You really are a tosser, Neil Pringle," she said over her shoulder.

A few minutes later they convened at Clayton's desk.

He looked up at them. "Right. Where do things stand with the Dead Pets' Society?"

Julie fished inside her bag and threw a furry baby seal at him. "Talking of dead pets, here's our new lucky mascot."

"Where did you get that?"

"St Valéry, of course," she said.

He plopped it onto the desk. It looked up at him adoringly, its head tilted just like Claire's.

They agreed that Clayton and Neil would interview Bob Jarvis, the nature reserve warden. Julie would go to Eddie's old school in case any of the teachers could tell them anything.

"And let's get the boyfriend in," said Clayton. "The shoe fits, just like Cinderella."

* * *

That afternoon, Julie drove to the school, which nestled in the shadow of the Glaveny church tower. Children were out in the schoolyard. She parked outside, and had reached the school gate before retracing her steps to double check that she'd locked the door and left the handbrake on. Were any of the kids watching? She felt foolish as she made her way through the yard.

The headmistress stood up from behind her desk to greet her. "We had some of your colleagues here last week to talk to the children about Road Safety week."

"I'm here about a more serious matter, I'm afraid. The murder of the waitress from the Point Hotel."

"I thought you'd just arrested somebody in France?"

"Yes, but we're also following up other leads. There is Jimmy Spratley's death too."

The headmistress' face darkened and her thick grey eyebrows drew together. "Yes. This is a very difficult time for the school."

"I'd like to ask the children about whether they might have been to the marsh just before Emma died. It could be vital for our investigation. How should I approach them?"

Miss Mallinson offered to introduce Julie to Eddie's teacher. She was a young woman in denim dungarees and sneakers.

"I'm here about the murder of Emma Dawson, Eddie Dawson's mother. I'd like to ask Eddie's old class whether any of them might have been on the marsh that day. We might need to set up meetings with their parents present."

"I'll draw you up a list. But they're resilient kids. They all went to the Lifeboat House not so long ago, and some of them got very interested in the bird migrations and the seals. Nature fires their imagination somehow."

Julie asked the teacher about Eddie.

"He was a bit of a loner. He did play with Jimmy Spratley, so the poor kid's not only lost his mum but his best friend as well. Thomas Sadler was his other friend. Thomas lives in Pelham and is a couple of years ahead of Eddie. It was quite unusual, as they usually stick with boys and girls of their own age. Thomas is always getting into scrapes. He wanders off on his own a lot."

"What lessons was Eddie particularly interested in?"

"He liked anything to do with nature — practical stuff. He was interested in prehistoric animals. He was an observer, and he was good at art too," the teacher said. "And he liked being outdoors."

Julie got Thomas Sadler's address from the headmistress. She'd have to ask for approval to interview him, but she knew that with her background in child protection, Bligh was unlikely to object. She was also unlikely to insist on the presence of a social worker or psychologist.

"How's Eddie doing?" the teacher asked.

"Not so well. He's still dumb with grief. But he's getting some art therapy."

"Really? He and his mother were very close. I hope he's going to be all right. It's tough for a child that age to come to terms with any death, never mind a murder. And his father wasn't around that much."

"Did the father come to parents' evenings, that sort of thing?" Julie asked.

"Rarely. He's in Norwich, I think. His mother was the one who came, but it was always difficult for her because of her job at the hotel."

* * *

Julie bought a ham sandwich in Glaveny village and ate it sitting in the car park which faced towards the North Sea. Clouds scudded across the horizon. As she chewed, she heard the ping of her phone. It was a text from Clayton with Bligh's approval for her interview with Thomas Sadler. Another child to interview. Julie realised she was struggling to maintain a professional distance in this case, and she knew why. It was too close to home.

Twelve years after burying her own child, she was still tortured by guilt. Her marriage hadn't survived the trauma of discovering Caroline, aged eighteen months, face down on the mattress in her room one morning. SIDS, that's what they called it, sudden infant death syndrome, and it had happened to her perfectly healthy toddler without warning. She would never forget that moment when she picked up her tiny body and turned her over. Then screamed. It was the first dead body she'd ever seen.

Even now, she dreamed about Caroline, and being reunited with her. Sometimes when she woke she could almost feel her in the room. Maybe that was why she was less sceptical than her colleagues about Emma and her contacts with another world. If she had just the slenderest chance of contacting her daughter, wouldn't she do it herself? She pushed the thought away, brushed the crumbs from her trousers and started the car.

Julie needed to collect herself. The trouble with this job was that she had no one to confide in. Not here. She reached the main road and as she turned left to Pelham she noticed St Nicholas church. What if she talked to the vicar about her troubles? She'd never been one for organised religion. But the vicar of Glaveny had to deal with death and bereavement all the time, just like she did. She checked the rear mirror. There was no one behind her. Her foot hovered between the brake and the accelerator for a few seconds. Then she drove on past the churchyard without another glance and down the hill towards Pelham.

She parked near the windmill and once more felt a strong urge to go back to the car and check the handbrake. What on earth is going on with me, she thought. All this fiddling about, checking things — the phone, the computer, the car. She remembered folding and refolding the towels at home. Could this be OCD? It's not a vicar I need, but a psychiatrist.

Instead of making her way to Thomas Sadler's house, she climbed up a grassy bank overlooking the marsh. The windmill's majestic white sails were still. She heard a voice behind her.

"The fret's coming in, see?" A birdwatcher, with a pair of binoculars swung round his neck, greeted her and went down the bank in his wellies.

She looked where he'd pointed, out towards the seal colony, and breathed in the salt air. A thick white shroud was forming and it was moving eastwards. This place seemed so tranquil, but then it could flip into a world of menace and foreboding just like that, she thought. The tall grasses rustling in front of her seemed to stretch all the way to the sea. Some black cows were huddled together in a rare patch of meadow. She heard invisible birds calling to each other across the creeks. Then, as she watched a flock of ducks flying in her direction in a perfect 'V,' she saw a thin figure emerging from the marsh. He was walking towards the windmill, and there was a big black dog running ahead of him. It was the hermit with the Great Dane.

She gasped and took a step back. Would the dog notice her? But its attention was focussed on a group of seagulls which it chased round in a circle. The man called out and held up a long leash. The dog galloped on. The hermit shouted out again, and this time Julie caught the words on the wind. "Caesar, come here!"

Julie stood still, watching the hermit attempt to capture the animal, his coat flapping in the breeze. The dog ignored the old man, obsessed with the gulls. She saw it leap up on its hind legs and grab a bird in its jaws, shaking it like a plaything. The other gulls scattered into the air, screeching. Caesar sank onto its haunches and pinned the bird to the ground with its paws. The dog was panting, drooling onto the grass. The hermit approached, holding out the leash, and he called again, "Come on, my Caesar." As the beast raised its head, he cast the slip-leash over its head like a lasso, then tried to pull the growling beast away from its lifeless prey.

The mist was almost upon them, its ghostly waves advancing steadily. Julie wanted to retrace her steps down the bank, but she remained motionless until the pair had moved down the path on the other side of the windmill, the seagull hanging from the dog's powerful muzzle.

* * *

The house she was looking for was at the far end of the village. The door was opened by a spotty, dark-haired boy wearing a baggy sweatshirt over a white T-shirt which hung over his jeans.

He looked at her suspiciously. "Yes?"

"You must be Thomas. Are your mum and dad in?"

"Mum's here."

A woman's voice called from inside. "Who's that?"

"Police, Mrs Sadler." The boy stepped aside to let her into the cottage. Somewhere a television was switched off. The living room was full of chintzy furniture and the shelves were cluttered with ornaments. A garland of Christmas lights curled round a collection of Toby jugs on the mantelpiece.

Tessa Sadler was a sturdy woman in her early thirties. A black bra gaped between two buttons of her shirt. "I'm sorry about that. Thomas is my guard dog."

Julie turned down the offer of a cup of coffee, and sat down, moving two satin cushions. The room was filled with the slightly sickly scent of candles.

Mrs Sadler sat down and stroked a leg in front of the electric fire. "Are you here about Emma Dawson? The whole village is distraught about her. I do the cleaning for three families, and they all told me so. Even the people at the big house." Her hand moved to touch a cross on a gold chain round her neck. "It's tragic it is. That girl was a good mother to Eddie. He was Thomas' best friend you know. And poor Jimmy Spratley. It's a terrible loss for the village. We joined the search when he went missing."

"It's actually Thomas I've come to see, in case he remembers anything that might be important for the investigation," Julie said.

The boy had disappeared to his room.

Mrs Sadler shouted from the bottom of the stairs. "Thomas! Come back downstairs again, will you? This lady wants to talk to you."

Thomas descended the stairs, dragging his feet.

Julie knew she had to be particularly cautious. Children could only be asked open questions, although she'd often been surprised by how talkative kids could be, even in a murder investigation. Not all of them were like Eddie, she thought. "Where did you and Eddie play together after school?"

He shrugged. "Depends. Sometimes here, sometimes at Eddie's house, sometimes with Jack next door, and sometimes on the marsh."

"And when were you last on the marsh?"

"The day before yesterday."

"It's just at the end of the road. The kids know it like the back of their hands," said his mother.

"And you don't worry about them going there on their own?"

"They're not alone, are they? There are always people around. And the wardens are there too."

"What about before Emma — Mrs Dawson — died? Did you go to the marsh then?"

He darted a look at his mother. "It were misty." He spoke in spurts, breathlessly. "And we saw Black Shuck!"

His mother looked at him sharply. "You saw Black Shuck? Never! Don't you tell lies now."

"We did, I swear. This big black dog came out of the mist. From the reeds. It were huge. It had huge eyes. And as soon as it saw Eddie, it turned away. It was him that made it go away."

"Who? Eddie?" Julie asked.

He nodded.

"Did you notice if Eddie behaved in a strange way after that?"

The boy began to fiddle with the bottom of his T-shirt. "Depends what you mean by strange. Quiet, yes."

"When did Eddie go quiet?"

"It was before that. A few days before Jimmy died. But I can't remember which day."

"So what do you think? Do you think Eddie saw something that made him go quiet? Or heard something?"

"I dunno."

"Do you know what Eddie did on the Saturday when his mum died?"

The boy frowned and bit his lip. "I think he said he were going for a walk with his mum, but I didn't want to go. It was misty."

"That's right. It was misty on that day. And do you remember where they went?"

"Maybe they didn't, I'm not sure. She had to work anyway. He didn't talk about it, like I said."

Julie was struggling to keep her voice as neutral as possible. "Thomas, Eddie hasn't said anything since his mum died. It's really important if you can remember anything at all. Did he say anything to you about what might have happened?"

"I told you already. He didn't say anything." His blue eyes were fixed on his mother.

After a moment, Mrs Sadler said, "I think that's enough. Is that alright?"

Julie looked reassuringly at Thomas. "Good boy, Thomas. That's very helpful."

But she had one last question. "You said you saw Black Shuck with Eddie. It doesn't sound as though he was afraid. Was Eddie afraid of anything?"

Thomas thought for a moment. "The hermit."

"Which hermit? The hermit of Pelham?"

The boy nodded. "I suppose so. I don't know any other one."

Julie recalled the scene she'd just witnessed on the marsh. "And you wouldn't have confused Black Shuck with the hermit's Great Dane?"

The boy shrugged. "Like I said, it was misty. When it's thick like that, you can only see shapes. And Eddie said it was Black Shuck!"

Interview over, Julie stepped outside into the cold, dank air. The mist had lifted and it was now drizzling. She sat in the car watching the windows steam up while she thought. Then she took out her phone and called Clayton.

"Boss, I've just had an idea."

The silence at the other end of the phone wasn't encouraging.

"Have we got any psychic mediums on our books? I think it's time we got one involved in this case."

Chapter 19

"Ahoy there!" The breeze picked up Neil's voice and carried it across the deserted car park at Branstable Quay, where the small boats rocked on the high tide.

They'd recognised the towheaded younger warden, who was talking to one of the boatmen on the quay. Skipper turned round and waved, and pointed towards the marsh. Clayton and Neil watched as a dark cloud rose and swept into the sky. They heard gunshots from their right, then saw two ducks fall to the ground. Two men, standing erect just across the creek, lowered their shotguns.

Neil approached the warden. "That's a bit close to the visitor centre, isn't it?"

"They have to go where the ducks are. With a storm coming and the wind picking up, it's a good day for hunting. I must admit, Bob and I aren't averse to a bit of wildfowling ourselves."

"Is he in today?" Clayton asked. It was his day off. Skipper walked back to the centre with them.

"Congratulations on the arrest."

"Thanks," said Clayton. "We're just following up some loose ends at the moment."

"What sort of loose ends?" Skipper pushed back his thick hair and waited.

He laughed when Clayton told him his colleague had been a regular at Emma's séances. "He's a dark horse, that one."

Clayton looked at him sharply. "What do you mean?"

"Nothing really. Just that he doesn't give much away. You know the other day when you came round to talk to us? Well, I probably shouldn't mention this but when he told me he had a migraine, I thought it was strange because he'd never mentioned suffering from them before. I thought that if you get migraines, it's a regular thing, right?"

"How long have you worked together?" Neil asked.

"The last three seasons. So we've spent quite a lot of time together. But he's worked here for longer. That's why he knows the locals. And he does a lot of the school talks."

"Do you socialise at all?"

"No. Not at all. Don't even go to the pub together. Sometimes I think he's avoiding me. He goes to the Harbour Inn, even though the King's Arms is just up the road, very close to where both of us live."

"Where's that?"

Skipper pointed up the lane, beyond the car park. "I've got a place on the main road in Branstable, with my old mum. Bob has one of the caravans in that field along there, the one closest to the entrance."

"When's his next shift?"

Skipper opened a drawer and took out their diary. He said that Bob had the weekend off, and wouldn't be back until Tuesday.

"Any idea what he's doing?"

"No idea. But I think he might be away." Skipper paused. "Is there anything else?"

"In fact there might be," said Clayton. He told the warden about the reports from St Valéry of people smugglers. "It's possible that they might be using Glaveny as an entry point for Ukrainian migrants," he said. "If so, it would be most useful if you could bear that in mind when you're out and about. Let's face it, if the seals can come round the coast on the tide, then why shouldn't people?"

"Why not indeed," said Skipper. "We'll keep our eyes peeled."

* * *

The two detectives left the Vauxhall in the car park and walked to the field indicated by the warden. There were six white caravans in a small caravan park opposite a farmhouse where chickens clucked in the yard.

The curtains were drawn at Bob Jarvis'. There was no car outside his or any of the other caravans.

"I'm going round the back," said Clayton.

Neil checked that the other caravans were vacant.

"Come over here," Clayton called out. He was peering through one of the back windows, whose curtains had been left open. Neil looked through the other one.

Inside, they could see a table and wraparound sofa seats. The kitchen counters were bare.

"You'd never think anyone lives here," said Neil, walking round to the other side. The bedroom curtains were drawn.

"Okay. Let's leave it for now," said Clayton. "Fancy a pint? The King's Arms is just across the main road."

As they left the caravan park, Clayton turned to face the estuary. He could see the spot where Emma Dawson's body had been piled into the boat on the quayside.

The two detectives ordered fish and chips at the bar and took their drinks to a small table.

"So, what about Julie's idea to contact a medium then?" Neil said. Clayton licked the white froth of his beer that he'd spilled onto his wrist. He could tell Neil had been waiting for this opportunity.

Neil picked up a fork and waved it in front of Clayton. "You are getting sleepy, *sleepy*."

Clayton laughed. "The boss has approved it. You know that we've used them before with missing persons. Can't do any harm, anyway. There's this woman in Norwich. I'm going to see her with Julie. Probably the whole thing will be a load of silly rubbish."

"And what about Skipper? The warden?" Neil said, pointing his thumb in the direction of the visitor centre.

"Could he be trying to put us off the scent? It's possible, I suppose." Their lunches had been brought to the table and Clayton was pouring vinegar over his chips.

"We never asked to see his tattoo," Neil said.

Clayton grinned. "So what if he goes to the Harbour Inn? Maybe he fancies the barmaid. I would, if I were him."

He took a sip of beer followed by a mouthful of batter which had just the right crispness. "But the timing is interesting. This migraine Jarvis supposedly had was on the Saturday afternoon. That's when Emma disappeared. He made sure Skipper knew about it so he'd have an alibi. What if Jarvis bundled her into his car and waited until dark before getting rid of the corpse?"

"But there were no tyre tracks at the scene," Neil said.

"He could have parked the car there. Might have just dragged her the last few yards or carried her over his shoulder. God, we were so lucky that the footprints weren't washed away by the rain. We'll come back on Tuesday and see what he has to say," he added. "That car of his might have a story for us."

Chapter 20

"The Old Town was the first place I explored when I moved here," Julie said.

"I obviously need to get out more," said Clayton. Was she doing this on purpose? "It's the first time I've been to Elm Hill."

Dombey & Son, the antiques store they were looking for, was halfway along the cobbled street. A bell rang as they pushed open the door of the timber-framed building, and an elderly man waved to them from a room in the back.

"Mrs Goddard?"

The man gestured to a narrow staircase winding upstairs. They made their way past mahogany tables, Victorian dolls and stacks of china.

"If you were a medium, don't you think you'd set up shop here too?" Julie whispered as they climbed the stairs.

Tina Goddard greeted them with a handshake. She led them into a small room lit by lamplight. Pictures of primeval forests and soaring mountains from middle earth looked down on them. A bookcase was jammed full of books on the occult. She led them to two armchairs, draped with shawls, in front of a low oval table on which a single overturned glass was placed. She sat between them, smoothed her skirt, then folded her hands.

"I worked with Jim Farrell, your predecessor," she said to Clayton.

His eyes were beginning to adjust to the gloom. "I saw that in the file."

"Yes, a girl who ran away from home. The body turned up in Hull. You're not from these parts, are you?"

"No. Preston."

"Is it nice round there?"

"Only if you like award-winning concrete bus stations."

Police work had been Clayton's ticket out of Preston. He'd left school at eighteen to escape his sister and joined the force in Manchester, where he'd applied to the CID. After he met Claire, he'd rarely taken her back to his home town, which was scarred by the scythes of city planners, but they'd often gone to the pubs in the outlying villages. That landscape has contours, he thought, not like here. And the people up north were definitely friendlier.

"Right, let's get down to business," said Tina Goddard.

Clayton opened his rucksack, took out a plastic bag and handed her a red woollen scarf. "You asked for something belonging to Emma Dawson. This was hers."

"And so I'm to try to contact Emma today, correct?"

"As you know, there have been two deaths in the space of a few days, one of them Emma Dawson, and we think they may be linked," Julie said. "Emma seems to have thought she had psychic powers, and her group certainly believed in them. She held séances during which she channelled Mother Julian."

"You don't think the teachings of Mother Julian had any connection with the murders, surely?"

The detectives said nothing.

"She's pretty famous round here. Her shrine is at the church just off King Street, it's only a few minutes' walk away. From what I've heard, she was a good woman."

"Yes, but she said that sin is necessary. And that you have to sin to be forgiven," Julie said. "Emma might have encouraged the people at the séances to carry out evil deeds for that reason."

Clayton sat back and watched the two women. Clearly Goddard wasn't buying Julie's theory.

The medium turned to Clayton. "There are plenty of evil spirits round here in Norfolk. Have you heard about Black Shuck?"

He rolled his eyes. "We most certainly have."

"Are we ready?" said the medium. "I would ask you both to concentrate on summoning Emma Dawson."

"Can we ask questions? We want to know what she saw. Maybe she knew the murderer."

"It's best that I take the lead." She sat up and picked up the scarf, unfolding it and pressing it to her face. She breathed deeply into its softness before letting it drop to her knees. Then she closed her eyes and stretched out a hand towards the glass.

She spoke in a clipped voice. "We are trying to contact Emma Dawson today. Is she there?"

The room was so still that Clayton could hear himself breathe.

"Emma Dawson?" the medium repeated. Her voice was even, respectful and welcoming. Still the glass did not move. After a few more minutes, she shook her head. Then, "Might Mother Julian be here today? Please signal to me if she is."

The hand on the glass remained immobile. Clayton's attention began to wander. A door behind the medium was ajar, and he could see a sink and a kettle on a counter. He wondered if she kept gypsy robes and a crystal ball stashed away in a cupboard to impress the customers. Today, though, she was dressed for the office.

Then she held up her hand. “Wait!”

Clayton’s gaze returned to her. She was frowning in concentration “The marsh,” she whispered.

Her other hand rested on the overturned glass. It moved sharply away from her, making Julie jump. Goddard’s eyes flew open, and her face seemed to crumple.

“Thank you, spirit, for your help,” she said, placing the scarf on the table. She got up and switched the light on. She seemed flustered.

“Would you like a glass of water?” Her forehead was damp. They both nodded, blinking, and watched her go into the kitchen.

Clayton could see her splashing her face with water. “What the fuck was that all about?” he said quietly to Julie.

“That thing with the glass scared me to death,” Julie said. She looked at her watch.

Goddard returned with three glasses on a tray, and set them on the table. She had regained her composure. Clayton gulped his water down. Julie was completely focused on the medium.

“I’m sorry about that. I’m afraid I couldn’t get hold of either Emma or Mother Julian. It’s not like a beauty contest, you know, where you pick them out of a line.”

“We understand,” said Clayton. “But what happened at the end?”

“Ah. Yes.” She looked at the glass on the table.

“I saw the marsh. I think it was the Glaveny marsh because I recognised the church tower. The spirit said that a child is going to die there.”

When they left Clayton shook his head and said, “Load of old rubbish.”

“Perhaps,” replied Julie.

Chapter 21

Julie parked her Clio outside the garage and noticed that the curtains in Ollie's room were still open. She sighed and checked her watch. It was past eight o'clock.

"Hi there! Sorry I'm late," she called out as she hung up her coat. She glanced into the living room. The babysitter was sitting next to Ollie on the sofa, where he was watching television in his pyjamas. The girl barely raised her head from her phone.

"Mummy! Where've you been?" He ran to her and she gathered him into her arms, smothering his cheeks with kisses. He's safe, she thought. He struggled to free himself.

"Busy day."

On their way back to the office she and Clayton had argued about the medium.

"Thank God you didn't offer to cross her palm with silver," she'd said, slamming the car door.

"Look at her track record," he fired back. "I checked the file before we came out and there was never any proof that she contributed to them finding that woman's body in Hull."

"There wasn't any proof that she didn't, either. The bottom line is that we've got to do everything in our power to prevent another murder right now, on our patch."

"Of course. But what do you suggest we do?"

"A curfew in Glaveny for one thing. Warn the school at the very least. Make sure the kids stay at home. The killer could strike again at any time."

"What, and cause panic across North Norfolk on the basis of one crazy lady who tells fortunes? Is that what you want, Julie? And what exactly would we tell them? That we've had a warning from a fucking medium? I can imagine the newspaper headlines already."

She'd sunk into the car seat, double checking that her phone was in her handbag. They drove in silence until they were pulling into the office car park.

"Okay. Look, why don't you have a quiet word with the headmistress?" Clayton had said. "You were probably going back to see her anyway, weren't you?"

She'd agreed, shooting him a hostile look. She knew exactly what he was driving at. Clayton thought she was taking this too personally. But he would never guess the reason why.

"Can I watch the end?" Ollie was saying to her. She followed him back to the sofa and covered his knees with a blanket, which he pulled up towards his face.

"That man's going to get it in the head!"

What the hell was he watching? The babysitter was collecting her things.

"Everything okay, Chloe?" she asked.

"He wanted to wait for you, Mrs Everett. I thought you wouldn't mind."

"What time does this finish?"

She shrugged. "Not sure. See you at the weekend?"

"Oh my God. We're supposed to be going to his dad's. I'd completely forgotten. I'll let you know." The babysitter slipped out of the front door, giving her a sympathetic smile.

"I'm just calling Daddy," she said to Ollie.

"Can't you wait? This is the best bit."

She'd had enough of this. She put the TV on mute and said, "You're going to bed, young man." Ignoring his shouts of protest, she passed him the phone. She watched his face while he chatted with his father. Paul was a detective who'd remained behind in Ipswich after she got the job in Norwich. They'd met while she was a child protection officer, still struggling to come to terms with Caroline's death. Paul had been such a comfort to her in those dark days. Friendship soon turned into something more. She thought of Caroline every day, even now, but she'd been so happy to discover she was expecting Paul's baby.

Watching Ollie now, she wondered whether she spoiled him because of what had happened to Caroline. She'd tried not to be overprotective, but he'd turned into a headstrong six-year-old, used to having his own way.

Ollie stood holding the phone defiantly, before handing it back to her. "We're going on Saturday."

She shook out her hair and went into the kitchen to speak to Ollie's dad. "I'm not sure about the weekend. You might have to come here instead. I've got so much work on, I'm knackered." Her voice cracked. It was only now, speaking to him, that she realised how stressed she was.

"I miss you," he said. "I want this to work, but sometimes I feel that it's too much for you."

"Please, Paul. Not tonight. Don't get heavy with me." She knew that after putting Ollie to bed she had more work to do. "I've got enough on my plate with a boss who's as sexist bully."

He laughed.

"Listen. He goes round kicking the office furniture and he seems to have decided I'm his punching ball. He doesn't like my approach to this case."

"He's not abusive with you, is he? Have you complained?"

"No and no. This is the police force, not a nursery."

"Well, suck it up then. But it's a pretty hair-raising case. I keep wondering when we'll be called in as reinforcements."

"And today a psychic predicted another child would die. It's too close to home, Paul, it really is."

She washed her hands, wiping the tap carefully with a tea towel afterwards, and took Ollie upstairs where he insisted on her playing a game with him on his tablet. The paintings on his bedroom wall reminded her of Eddie's drawings. Yawning, she went back downstairs where she tidied the living room, plumping the cushions one by one, before switching on her laptop.

Was that Goddard woman a fraud? Maybe she'd been too gullible. In that case, what about Emma Dawson? Was she for real? How could she have deceived so many people?

She googled 'hypnosis.' According to one medical article she found, it was only effective with people who wanted to be hypnotised. So if you resisted, Julie thought, it didn't work. Hypnosis subjects had to feel comfortable and relaxed. That's why Emma Dawson was so successful, she thought. She was able to play mind games because they *wanted* to play.

She rested her head in her hands and stared at the screen. She heard a faint movement from above. Ollie was sitting at the top of the stairs, his toes poking through the banister. Is that where Eddie has sat while his mother contacted the dead? Could it be that he was trying to express something in the drawings that Clayton had ridiculed?

"I can't get to sleep," Ollie mumbled.

"Just coming," she said, and closed the laptop. She walked slowly up the stairs. What if it was Eddie who held the key to the murder?

She followed Ollie into the bedroom and wrapped the duvet around him. She leaned over to give him a kiss.

"Why are you working so late?"

"This is a big case. It's hard to crack. I was just thinking about a little boy who might be able to help us."

"What little boy?"

"Oh you don't know him. His name's Eddie."

"Not Eddie whose mum was murdered? Eddie Dawson? He's in my class."

Julie's mouth fell open. Why had it never crossed her mind that he might have transferred to the same school as Ollie in Norwich? Both of them were the same age, it stood to reason they'd be in the same class.

"How's he getting on?" she asked.

"He's weird. He never says anything. He's really shy or something. Some of the boys in my class are horrible to him in the playground."

"I hope you're not one of them, sweetie. He should be your friend. He's going through a tough time."

She kissed him goodnight, put out the light and went downstairs to check that she'd switched off the computer.

I'll just read one more article, she thought to herself, switching it on again. She went back to googling 'hypnosis.'

After a few minutes, she glanced upstairs in case Ollie had got out of bed again. But she saw no one in the shadow cast by the standard lamp. What could Eddie have seen or heard that he was trying to tell them?

She decided it was time to call it a day.

Chapter 22

Neil caught the vinegary smell of moist laundry clinging to the farmhand's body as they went into the interview room.

He gave his name as Jason Mellor, and his address as Oak Farm. He was twenty-eight.

"We're following up on my chat with you at the farm. We're carrying out background checks regarding the murder of Emma Dawson. This is DI Clayton."

Mellor pushed back his chair. "You mean I'm a suspect in Emma's murder? Should I get a solicitor?"

"That is your right of course, but like I said, we're just doing background checks. Now I want you to think back to Saturday, November first. Where were you on that day?"

"Working. Digging up beets on the farm."

"Can someone vouch for you on that?" Neil asked.

"Sure. My boss."

"And what about that evening?"

"I went down the pub, the Harbour Inn."

"Why there?"

"Jen's there. Hub of the universe."

"What? Her, or the pub?"

"Both, really," said Mellor.

Clayton chipped in. "But we understood that you were rather keen on Emma Dawson?"

"What of it?"

It was Neil's turn. "Where did you first meet Mrs Dawson?"

"It would've been at the pub. We were introduced by Jen Draper, the barmaid at the Harbour Inn. She knew her from before, and then Emma came back to Glaveny to work at the Point Hotel."

Clayton leaned forward. "If you were in a relationship with Emma Dawson, why didn't you see her on the Saturday night?"

Mellor examined his hands, roughened by manual work. "No comment."

Clayton leafed through a printout on the table. "You rang her though, on the day she died. What was that phone call about?"

Mellor looked up. "Do I need a lawyer?"

"Your choice, Mr Mellor."

"She cheated on me," he mumbled.

Neil glanced at the tape recorder. "Could you repeat that a little more loudly?"

Mellor repeated his words.

"And could you be a little more explicit?" added Clayton.

"I found out she'd been sleeping with that French guy, didn't I?"

"Found out?"

"Someone in the pub saw them together. Small place — Glaveny." He stiffened. "Then I saw him in the pub on Halloween, and I lost it."

"How did you lose it?"

Mellor smiled grimly. "I took him outside and I gave him a piece of my mind. Or a piece of my fist."

The two detectives glanced down at the hands resting on the table. "Were there any witnesses?"

"We went round the back, so I don't think so."

"How did he react?"

"He hit back, of course. But he said he didn't know about me and Emma."

"And you didn't see Mrs Dawson at all the day after the fight, which would be the Saturday, right?" Neil said.

Mellor shook his head. "That's right."

"Just the phone call. But you might also have gone round to her place to have it out with her. Or you might have bumped into her somewhere."

Mellor raised his voice, and pointed a finger at Neil. "You said when you called that I was to come in on a voluntary basis. I've got nothing more to say."

"One more question, if we may?" said Clayton. "It's about the séances. I'd really like to know how a grown man like you could be persuaded to slit the throat of a harmless animal."

Mellor scratched his forehead. "I've thought about that myself quite a bit. It was like a club. Everyone liked Emma and trusted her. Like I just told you, I was particularly close to her."

"And what was the atmosphere like there?"

"Atmosphere? Well, come to think of it, it was always chilly in her house when we went. I wondered whether she'd turned the heating off before we got there. And sometimes there was a kind of breeze inside the house, a draught I suppose you'd call it. It gave me a buzz to think we were in contact with Mother Julian. When she suggested we all get tattoos we felt like we belonged to a secret society. It's not any worse than the Freemasons, is it?"

Clayton was grim. "We're talking about a murder!"

"Well, it's not me that did it. I told you, that's enough." He stood up to leave.

Neil watched him go. "Shit, we've got more suspects in this case than I've had hot dinners."

"I'm going to call Gallois in St Valéry and let him know about the punch up. I'll see what's going on over there. A love triangle puts this murder in a whole new light," said Clayton.

Chapter 23

Bob Jarvis usually enjoyed his trips to Holt, where he'd often bump into tourists who'd been to the Glaveny reserve. It made him feel like a local celebrity. In fact he *was* a local celebrity. The tourists were scarce now, but plenty of the locals recognised him from the marsh tours he'd given them or their children in the past few years.

He had to get the car cleaned, but otherwise he had no particular plans and a long weekend ahead of him. Skipper wasn't expecting him back until Tuesday. He strolled along the High Street, looking in the shop windows. He checked his appearance in the window of the kitchenware store. He stared at the exorbitant prices of the goods inside.

"Morning, Bob."

He Jarvis turned round abruptly. It was the new boatman from Branstable.

"Hello there," he said, shaking the man's hand. "I'm sorry but I've forgotten your name."

"Woodford. Steve Woodford. We met at Emma's that time."

"Of course. Yes. Steve. What brings you to Holt?"

"I'm going to get myself a tattoo, like the rest of you." Woodford was older than Jarvis, with a long, shaggy beard.

"Ah, so you want to belong."

"Community, isn't it? It would be nice to see the redheaded barmaid again too. She's ready for her close-up, isn't she? How long have you been in the group?"

Jarvis bridled at the reference to Jen. He racked his brains for an excuse to walk away. "Oh, a fair bit. Now, if you don't mind, I've got a few things to do here. Better get on."

"You got family here?"

Jarvis forced himself to smile. "No, actually. Anyway, see you around."

As he walked away, Woodford said, "Yes, see you at the next one."

He didn't look back.

* * *

Immediately he walked into the Pizza Express, Clayton spotted Claire. Seated at a table by the large windows, she hadn't noticed him and was checking her makeup in a powder compact.

He studied her from the door. She looked radiant. She stowed the compact in her large black handbag and looked towards the entrance. She caught sight of him as he walked towards her and stood up. They kissed awkwardly — he missed her cheek and planted a kiss on her ear. He inhaled her familiar perfume.

He gestured to her glass of white wine. "I see you've started without me."

They ordered. The restaurant was filling up. Sam told her about his trip to St Valéry and the frustrations of the Glaveny murder case. Claire went into too much detail about her hospital work. They hadn't talked so much when they were together.

"How's the house?" she asked.

"Could be tidier," he said, and she smiled. "Actually, I'm thinking about getting a smaller place." Why had he said that? He didn't want her to think he was hard up after buying out her share of the house when they'd divorced. "I mean, move closer to work," he said. He'd never minded the half-hour drive to the nick when they were together. She'd been the one to insist on living in the city because of her job. Norwich's Notting Hill, as she called their neighbourhood of Victorian terraced houses. But she no longer ruled his life, did she?

"The neighbours still think they're Motorhead?"

"Bloody students." He moved his beer glass aside and the waiter put down his pizza. They ate their food in silence, catching each other's eye from time to time, and looking away with a smile.

"So, have you been dating?"

He twisted a strand of mozzarella round his fork without replying. He felt resentment fizzing inside him. Why should he give her the satisfaction of knowing that she hadn't been replaced, and never could be?

She finished her wine. They admired the view of the church outside, lit up in the dark. Clayton found himself thinking about Mother Julian, whose shrine was somewhere in Norwich.

His phone rang in his jacket pocket. He fumbled behind the chair to fish it out. It was a number he didn't recognise.

"Detective Inspector? It's Mike Skipper here, the warden."

"Sorry, love, got to take this." Clayton walked to the restaurant entrance.

"What's up, Mr Skipper?"

"I'm sorry to bother you on a Saturday night, but I'm calling about the matter of the Ukrainians that you mentioned. I think I saw a boatload arriving today. I'm sorry I've left it until now to call you, but . . ."

"What time did you see them?"

"About four thirty this afternoon. It was just starting to get dark. At first I thought it was a regular boat trip, but it wasn't the right time of day for them. There was a light guiding them in, but they didn't come to Branstable and must have beached in a channel somewhere."

"Could you get out in daylight tomorrow and have a look? I'll send someone down to check it out."

By the time he'd zigzagged through the restaurant back to his seat, Claire had finished. She never ate her pizza crust. Clayton noticed a trace of pink lipstick on her napkin, by the side of her plate. "Did you hear about Simon and me?"

He tried to swallow a piece of pizza which for some reason had stuck in his throat.

"It's over," she said.

"That didn't last long." Clayton was suddenly struck by an inexplicable fear. Did she want them to get back together again? He wasn't ready for it, yet wasn't it what he'd wanted? He held up a hand. "Don't tell me any more. I don't want to know."

The waiter took their plates. "Dessert?"

Clayton shook his head.

"Do you fancy a coffee, Sam?"

"No thanks, I'm fine." Clayton asked for the bill. "That was a work call. I'd better go."

He paid the bill, over her objections, and they stepped out into the clear night. Suddenly he noticed her high heels. He was in jeans as usual, but she'd dressed up for the occasion.

Outside, they said goodbye. Out of the corner of his eye Clayton could see a gang of beggars approaching to ask for spare change. He took her arm and steered her away.

"Keep in touch," she said, leaning to kiss him. He turned so that she pecked his cheek. She reached up to raise his jacket collar, and tightened the scarf around his neck. He let her do it.

He escorted her to the nearest bus stop and looked at his watch. It would take him less than half an hour to walk home. He set off, humming the tune from *Romance.*

Chapter 24

"Sorry to bother you on a weekend, guv."

Clayton recognised Julie's voice and waited for the word "but."

"But I've been thinking about Eddie," Julie said.

"Haven't we all?" Another Sunday afternoon ruined.

"This might be a bit off the wall, but we know he was upstairs when some of these séances took place. What if he wasn't asleep and heard what was going on? What if he heard what Emma was telling them to do after she hypnotised them? He might be able to identify the culprit."

Clayton sighed. He kicked off his flip-flops and fell back heavily onto the sofa.

"You're obsessed with bloody psychics! We're starting to get more promising leads now, you know."

"Yes, but I'm just saying. Number one, we might be able to prevent another murder, and number two, have we paid enough attention to Eddie's pictures? I've been thinking about it, and I wonder whether those drawings are a depiction of Jimmy Spratley's murder, for a start. Think about it. What if he saw or heard something, and that's what he's trying to tell us through his drawings."

"Okay, so what do you want?"

"What about seeing whether Eddie would take part in a séance?"

Clayton snorted. "A six-year-old child? We'd never get permission for it!"

"We might if we could persuade his dad. And Eddie might agree if he thought he'd be able to contact his mum."

Clayton looked wistfully at his music stand. Then out of the window. They might persuade Eddie's dad, but what about the others? "Can't do any harm to ask, I suppose. What time can you get down there? I'll meet you."

* * *

Julie went into her living room, where Paul and Ollie were playing a video game. "You okay to stay until I get back? I've got to go to work for a bit."

Paul followed her into the hall. "What's going on? You know I've got to get back to Ipswich tonight."

"Yes. I'm sorry, but it's this case. There's a kid involved and I need to make sure we're doing the right thing."

"There's a kid involved here too, Julie. Don't forget that." He turned away.

"I'll ring you!"

But he'd gone.

* * *

Brian Dawson came to the door with a bottle of ale in one hand and the TV remote in the other.

He led Clayton and Julie into the living room. Clayton recognised the light blue of Man City on the TV. His team was playing Southampton.

"You support them or the Saints?" Clayton said, gesturing.

"I'm a Canaries fan," said Dawson, hitting the mute button. "Always supported the local team. Mind, we lost to Reading yesterday afternoon."

Dawson was clearly itching to return to the match. Clayton would have happily joined him but said, "I'm sorry to bother you and Mrs Dawson again, but we'd like to see Eddie if that's possible."

Dawson looked bewildered.

"Eddie?" he said.

Julie stepped forward. "We've been studying those pictures of Eddie's, and we need to follow up. We think he might be the key to his mother's death. In fact, we're hoping that you can persuade him to talk to us about what he might have heard or seen."

Dawson looked from one to the other, then at Caitlin who was standing by the door. "I thought you had the guy that did it?"

"It's important, actually. We're still trying to nail down some stuff in the case." Clayton's eyes were drawn to the screen. The score was two-nil to Man City, he noted with satisfaction.

Caitlin called out, "I told you that boy's got second sight." She disappeared into the next room and came back with a picture. "Here's another one he did."

It showed a halo in the sky and a face surrounded by lines of white chalk.

Clayton recognised the woman in the headdress from Emma Dawson's cottage. "It's Mother Julian!"

Julie flashed him a triumphant look.

There was a tower in the foreground that looked like part of a church. St Nicholas? Or was it in Norwich? Two stick figures, holding hands. Eddie and his mother? But they weren't standing on the ground. They seemed to be flying towards the sky with a flock of birds.

Clayton peered at it. "We're trying to figure out how much Eddie knew about his mother's séances. It could be vital information for the investigation."

“Séances? That’s the first I’ve heard about it. Are you saying my son was mixed up in that rubbish? That’s the last thing he needs.”

“Not directly, of course not,” said Clayton. “But he may have heard or seen something during one of the sessions. From upstairs, that is.”

Dawson said, “You do realise he’s only six, don’t you? Six.”

Julie fixed him with a stare. “Mr Dawson, my own child is six, exactly the same age as Eddie. If I felt that he might be able to help solve a murder, believe me I wouldn’t hesitate to ask him.”

Dawson turned to Caitlin.

“I’ll make us all some tea,” she said.

“I’ll see if he’ll come down,” said Dawson reluctantly. “He and Lauren are playing up there.”

Fifteen minutes passed. Caitlin brought in tea on a tray. “Do you want to watch the match?” Clayton did.

She turned up the sound. “It’s lucky you didn’t come yesterday. You wouldn’t have found him in a good mood then. Norwich lost two-one.”

They heard Dawson coming down the stairs. He was shaking his head. “He won’t do it. I told you.”

Julie looked at Clayton then said, “If we gave you a bit more time to persuade him, maybe he might talk to me tomorrow? I’ll see if I can draw him out. It would give us time to get clearance. ”

Dawson still had one eye on the TV. “I still don’t see why he’d talk to you.”

“I’ll see whether Becky Berry, and possibly Jen Draper, might be free to come along. He might feel more comfortable in their presence,” Julie said.

Dawson seemed to be weighing his decision, frowning. “Come back tomorrow evening, and we’ll see. But I can’t promise anything.”

Julie thanked Caitlin for the tea and the two detectives walked outside to their cars.

"What are you cooking up now?" Clayton asked, as her car door clicked open.

"Nothing. Why?"

Chapter 25

The white motorboat was big enough to hold ten to fifteen people. Skipper had found it beached in the mud a few hundred yards from the quay.

"We'll impound this boat," Neil said. "The people smugglers must be working with a local contact." Before the warden returned to the information centre, Neil asked for the boatman's name.

"There are a few of them. But you'll probably only find a couple at this time of year. Steve Woodford lives near here, along the road from the boat tours office. Wait a sec, I'll draw you a map."

Neil texted Clayton to say he'd follow up with the boatman about the séances. He'd leave the migrants for the immigration police. No point queering their pitch. A few minutes later, he was parking outside a whitewashed cottage. He rang the bell.

The door creaked, opening to reveal a tall, bearded man. A nest of blue veins curled around the tip of his bulbous nose.

"Mr Woodford?"

He nodded.

"DS Neil Pringle, Anglian CID. May I come in?"

Woodford held the door open. Neil brushed past coats and waterproofs hanging from a hook on the wall. There were a couple of pairs of wellingtons by the door.

"Your name's come up in connection with Emma Dawson, the waitress from the Point. She was murdered on the marsh the day after Halloween." He was bluffing but it was worth a try. "How well did you know her?"

"Not that well. I only met her a few times."

"The séances, right?"

Woodford seemed startled. "Who's been telling you about that?"

Neil continued. "And what were *you* asked to do? Strangle a pet, perhaps?" Or carve the heart out of an eight-year-old boy.

"So you're investigating the murder of poodles now as well?"

Neil changed tack. "Perhaps you could tell me where you were on the weekend of November first?"

"I'd have to check. That was a while ago."

"Out with the boat? Did you see anything suspicious on the Sunday?

"Oh, that's the weekend, isn't it? I was away then. My mother's sick."

"And where's she?"

"Peterborough. When I came back the next day, it was all over the papers."

"You've got a receipt or train tickets for your journey?"

"I don't believe I kept them. But my mother would vouch for me."

"What time did you get back?"

"Let's see." He stroked his beard. "It was late on the Sunday. About ten in the evening, I reckon."

"Presumably you'd have taken Emma Dawson out on the boat a few times?"

"That's right. Nice woman. She'd go seal watching, counting pups, that sort of thing."

"Can you remember the last time you saw her? Did she seem worried at all?"

"It may have been down the Harbour Inn. But we didn't talk. She went back to her place with Jen the barmaid, I think. Seemed happy enough."

Neil took down Woodford's phone number and turned to go. "What size shoe do you take?"

"Eight and a half. What's it to you?"

Near enough to nine, Neil thought. "Got hiking boots as well as these wellingtons?"

"Of course."

"How many pairs?"

"Two."

Neil shut his notebook. "We may need you to come to the station." He turned to go. The boatman slammed the door shut behind him.

Chapter 26

Brian Dawson heard footsteps on the path and looked through the front door window. He saw three shapes illuminated by the outdoor light. Here come the three witches, he thought.

Julie stepped forward, followed by Becky Berry. Dawson didn't know the third woman.

Becky held out her hand. "Nice to see you again, Mr Dawson."

He nodded and invited them inside. They stood in the hall, as though waiting for instructions.

He turned to the redhead. "Are you the psychologist?"

"I'm Jen Draper. From the pub."

Julie spoke up. "They said I didn't need to bring a psychologist, as I was in child protection before. We didn't want to crowd Eddie."

"Caitlin's gone out with Lauren and the boy's upstairs. But I can tell you now, he's not saying anything."

"We'll go up then. Don't worry about us," Julie said. Dawson went back into the living room, shaking his head, and switched on the television.

* * *

The bedroom door was closed, and Julie knocked softly before she opened it. Eddie was sitting on the floor, resting against the bed, and fiddling with some sort of plastic robot. He jumped up when he saw Becky Berry, who entered the room behind her.

"You lovely boy, how are you? I've missed you," she said, wrapping her arms round him.

He allowed her to cuddle him. Julie saw that his body was heaving.

"You remember Jen, don't you? And the nice lady from the police? May we sit down with you?"

They settled on the floor in a circle. The curtains were closed, and the room was lit dimly by a bedside light. As they'd agreed, Julie let Becky take the lead.

Becky continued. "I hear you've been doing some drawings. May we have a look?"

Eddie put down his toy and went to the chest of drawers. He picked up a pile of papers, handed them to Becky, and sat down again, hugging his knees.

She sifted through the pages, putting them one by one on the floor. Julie recognised most of them as the pictures Dawson had brought to the office.

Becky pointed to the cat with its hair standing on end. "That's Max, isn't it? He's mad, isn't he? We've taken him in, but he's a handful. And the dog. Is that Black Shuck?"

He nodded. Julie saw that ever so slightly, the hands around his knees seemed to be loosening. "I've been talking to your friend, Thomas. He told me that you saw Black Shuck on the marsh. He was very impressed by how you sent it away. He doesn't have the same special powers as you."

Eddie said nothing. His eyes were fixed on the drawings. Becky held up the one with a stick figure on the marsh and the smudge of a body at its feet. It must be the murder of Jimmy Spratley, thought Julie, feeling her skin prickle. Becky put it down and they all studied it.

"You must miss Mummy so much," Becky said. "We were thinking that we might try to contact her tonight. If that's okay with you?"

Was this too soon, Julie thought, scarcely daring to breathe.

Becky reached towards him to give him a hug. Again, he didn't resist, his curls flopping over his forehead. "Let's hold hands like we used to do with Mummy. Jen, you can start if you like."

They locked hands, Becky was on one side of Eddie with Jen Draper on the other, and Julie completed the circle. The painting of the murder on the marsh lay in the centre, next to the plastic robot.

Jen began. "Emma, Emma, are you there?"

They waited, their shadows swaying on the wall. Julie was reminded of their session with the medium. Maybe this wasn't such a good idea after all.

Eddie broke the silence. He said in a whisper, "It's me." He seemed to be listening. A moment later, a beatific smile crossed his face. Something powerful was happening. He lifted his face towards the ceiling as though he could see something. Could he be putting on an act? Julie wondered, then dismissed the thought.

Jen Draper was speaking again. "Emma? What did you see? What can you tell us?"

Eddie was looking at the ceiling. Then he began squirming, as though trying to escape something. He pulled a hand away and held it up in front of his eyes. He seemed to be fighting with something.

"Don't!" he cried out.

Eddie took his other hand from Jen's and placed it on his neck. "Here?" he asked. Then he let out a low moan, "Mummy, Mummy." Then he was still. The boy blinked.

"What did you see?" Becky asked gently.

"I saw Mummy being killed," he said, and began to sob.

"Did you see who did it?"

Eddie nodded.

Chapter 27

The three women looked at one another, afraid to break the spell.

"Do you know the person?" Julie asked, gently.

Eddie nodded again, wiping his tears with one hand.

"Who was it?"

He looked as though he was on the point of speaking, but then fell silent.

Shit, Julie thought. We were so close. The boy sat staring at the drawing on the floor, rubbing his eyes. After a few moments, Becky gave him a hug and patted his knees.

"Well done, Eddie. You did really well. Your mummy would be proud of you. We'll get your daddy now."

He picked up his toy and cradled it. Raising his other hand, he put his thumb in his mouth.

"We'd better be off. I'll see you again soon. We'll arrange some play days with Jack," said Becky. "I'll ask your daddy about a sleepover. Would you like that?"

At the mention of his friend's name, Eddie took his thumb out of his mouth. "Yes, please," he said.

* * *

Clayton saw Julie making her way towards him. He picked up the toy seal and waved to her with its flipper.

"Great job, Julie. Bloody good. So the boy knows the murderer. We'll just get some photos and pics together and take them round."

She spoke without thinking. "So much for old-fashioned police work then. It's the child psychic who solves the case."

He put down the seal and looked at her strangely. "What do you mean, child psychic? I thought you women convinced him to talk to you."

"It's not actually that simple."

"Jesus fucking Christ! You're not telling me you held a séance with a six-year-old boy without the approval of your senior officer?"

She could feel the flush creeping up her neck. "I wouldn't call it a séance exactly. It was kind of informal."

"But you know the rules about interviewing children."

She bridled. "I'd remind you that I'm the one with child protection experience. We've achieved a breakthrough here."

He stood up and came round to her side of the desk, bringing his face close to hers. She stood her ground. Don't you dare threaten me, she thought.

"Well, that remains to be seen. I was surprised that his psychologist agreed to the interview. Now you're telling me she didn't know anything about it!"

"No. But we did get the father's consent. And I talked things over with Becky and Jen, who were as sensitive as possible. I thought it was best that they took the lead because of their relationship with Eddie."

Before Clayton could say any more she said, "I'll brief the psychologist and the social worker today. Maybe I won't mention the word séance though. The key thing is that we achieved our objective, and Eddie is starting to speak again. I think he'll be fine. He has a loving relationship with his dad, he's spoken to his mum, or at least he thinks he has. And, last but not least, he's recovered the power of speech."

Clayton's jaw tightened. "This could backfire, you know. I'm going to have to cover for you, you do realise that?"

"Yes. Sorry. I thought it was worth it, that's all."

His expression softened. "I know. Point taken." He wasn't about to admit that he might have done the same thing himself.

Neil appeared, holding three cups of coffee. Was it that time already?

"Come on, Neil, there's no time to lose. We've got to get some pictures together to take to the Dawsons. Julie, you're staying here."

She took her coffee and went back to her desk, tears stinging her eyes.

* * *

It was lunchtime by the time Clayton and Neil arrived in Glaveny.

Clayton was relieved that it was Caitlin who answered the door. She told them she'd kept Eddie at home for the day.

"How is he?"

"Actually, he seems to be back with us at long last, Inspector. Maybe he got a lot out of his system last night," she said.

"Good. Is Mr Dawson in?"

"He's at work. Do you want to come in?"

"We just need to follow up with Eddie on one small thing. It'll only take a few minutes, if you don't mind."

They found Eddie watching television in the living room.

"Hello, son. Do you want to play a game with us?" said Clayton. It's called hunt the murderer, he added silently.

Eddie cleared a space and Clayton sat on the sofa next to him. Neil found an armchair and began spreading photos and drawings on the coffee table in front of them, dealing them out like a pack of cards.

Speaking very gently, Clayton said, "Do you remember last night when the nice ladies asked you who you'd seen with your mummy when she died? All you have to do is point to the one you saw. Just pick them up one by one and have a look."

Neil picked up the remote. "Let's switch off the TV, so you can concentrate." He picked up the first picture, an artist's impression of the hermit of Pelham. The dark eye patch was clearly visible.

"Is this the man you're afraid of?"

Eddie shook his head. The boy picked up the next one, with Clayton looking over his shoulder. It was the boatman, Steve Woodford. The boy cast it aside. He looked at the others, and all produced the same reaction. He shook his head at Len the painter, and Mike Skipper the warden. There was only one picture left — Skipper's colleague, Bob Jarvis.

They hadn't brought any pictures of women. But Clayton dismissed the thought. Most women wouldn't have had the strength to move Emma's body.

He could almost feel his heart beating. "Last one."

The boy picked up the photo and gasped. He stared at it for a long time.

"It's him," the boy said.

Clayton noticed his hand trembling as he set the photo down again. "You're sure?"

Eddie looked up at him and nodded.

"Good boy!"

Clayton went to look for Caitlin, who was in the kitchen chopping onions.

"We're finished here. Take care of him. He's done really well."

They gathered the documents together, Neil almost forgetting his jacket in his eagerness to get out.

"Jarvis was away until today. Fingers crossed that he's at work," Clayton murmured as they left. "Skipper might have tipped him off."

Chapter 28

Neil got the siren going as they got into the Vauxhall. "No harm in letting them know we're coming."

"Stop that," said Clayton. "It's not an emergency — yet. It'll take us almost an hour to get there anyway."

He checked his watch. "We'll try the visitor centre first. It's a pity we didn't go there first thing."

"They might be out on the marsh by now," Neil said. "It's not as though they'll put on a welcoming party."

The tyres squealed as Clayton turned into the car park at Branstable Quay. He pulled up sharply and they began running towards the wooden cabin. Skipper and Jarvis were standing at the entrance in the winter sunshine. They saw Skipper say something to Jarvis, and then everything happened in a rush.

Jarvis ran inside and reappeared brandishing a shotgun. He grabbed hold of Skipper with the other hand.

"Jesus Christ! Look at the size of that thing," Neil said quietly.

Clayton shouted out to Jarvis. "Don't be a fool! We're taking you in for questioning about the murder of Emma Dawson. Don't make your situation worse."

Jarvis raised the gun. "Stay where you are! If you come any closer, he gets it."

The younger warden's eyes were wide with fear. Jarvis stumbled down the stairs with his hostage and began dragging him towards the jetty.

Clayton and Neil stood there with their arms hanging at their sides.

Jarvis half marched, half dragged Skipper towards the wardens' grey rubber dinghy moored at the quay. He pushed him aside and jumped down into the boat, out of sight. Skipper fell onto the jetty with a crack.

Clayton and Neil began sprinting towards the boat. A moment later they heard the sound of the motor and saw the vessel zig-zagging out of the marina. Jarvis was holding up the gun.

"Fuck! Fuck!" shouted Clayton, startling two fly fishermen in chest waders who were unloading their catch.

Neil ran back to the visitor centre and climbed up to the observation tower to follow Jarvis' escape. "He's gone towards the seal colony! Come on, let's go." He came back down the stairs two at a time and went into the centre.

Clayton turned his attention back to the jetty. "Can anyone help us with a boat?"

"What are you after?" the boatman asked.

Neil emerged a moment later, holding up a pair of binoculars and made his way to the quayside. Clayton was yelling at a boatman who had just returned from a seal trip. Skipper picked himself up and climbed into the boat with the detectives, just as the boatman switched on the engine.

Clayton indicated Skipper. "This man's colleague."

"No kidding?"

The boat was unsteady as it pulled away from the quay. "Can't this thing go any faster?"

"It's built for more people," the boatman said. They crested the swell of the open sea where the wind was gusting. They began to realise that they didn't have a hope in hell of catching up with the dinghy.

Clayton gestured in the direction of Glaveny Point. “Head for the seals!” He sat down, almost missing the seat, to text DCI Bligh. Neil was standing, scanning the darkening horizon with the binoculars.

“What on earth did you say to him?” Clayton said to Skipper, as quietly as he could over the sound of the motor and the whistling wind.

“I just told him that you said you’d be back. I guess he must have panicked. Sorry.”

The boat came round the spit, followed by a couple of frolicking grey seals. They dived, disappearing from view, and then resurfaced, seeming to smile at them. No sign of the warden.

Clayton took the binoculars, scrutinising the ebbing tide and the marsh. He saw the seal pups crowded onto the shingle. Jarvis could be anywhere. He knew the marsh’s secret places and inlets better than anyone.

“What do you think?” he said to Skipper, who was rubbing his leg on the seat.

“He might have taken the Pelham channel towards the ruined chapel. He could ditch the boat anywhere along there. But if it were me, I’d head for the open sea and then go east along the coast towards Sheringham.”

Clayton sat down again heavily. “Take us back.”

Chapter 29

Thomas Sadler got off the bus and walked towards his house in Pelham. He had at least two hours before his mother returned from work. Ever since Jimmy died and Eddie had moved, he'd been at a loss for what to do.

He let himself in as usual, and went upstairs to play a video game. But it didn't hold his attention and he went back downstairs. A few minutes later, he closed the door behind him and unlocked his bicycle. He cycled along to the pottery store, where Mrs Marshall was arranging artificial flowers in a vase.

"Hello, Thomas. Are you looking for Jeremy?"

"Can he come out to play?"

"He's with Jack in Glaveny this afternoon," she said. "We could've fixed up something earlier, but he won't be back before supper time now. Everything alright?"

"Fine."

"Well, don't stay out after dark."

He drifted along the High Street and turned onto Beach Road towards the sea. There were reed beds on either side of the narrow road. He picked up a stick and began thwacking the roadside weeds with one hand while pedalling along. He stopped to watch a flight of Canada geese taking off from a pond in formation, honking as they passed over him. He heard a car slow down behind him.

"Afternoon, Tom. Where are you off to?" It was one of the neighbours. He could see their black Labrador caged at the back of the estate car.

"Hello, Mrs Rogers. Just going to see the baby seals."

"What, on your own? Does your mum know?"

He shook his head. "I'll be home before she gets back."

"Well, take care, and don't go too far." She rolled up the window, said something to her husband and rolled it down again. "We're taking the dog to Pelham. Do you want to come with us?"

"No thanks, Mrs Rogers, I'm going the other way."

"You sure?"

Thomas nodded and waved goodbye with his stick. He followed the car to the beach car park and saw them start walking in the direction of Pelham. He dropped his bike on the shingle and began the trudge in the opposite direction towards the seal colony. He turned to face the north-westerly wind which was blowing wisps of mist towards him. His energy was beginning to flag. Would he have time to get to the seal spit before having to turn back? It was a four-mile round trip to the Point.

He hadn't seen the pups since before Jimmy died. But he couldn't remember it being so far. Maybe this time it seemed further away because he was on his own.

He missed Eddie. His conversation with the policewoman had brought back memories of the times they'd gone exploring the marsh, its bird hides and abandoned boats. They'd pretended they were pirates or hunting for buried treasure. Sometimes they'd found birds' eggs. A lot of the time their mothers had thought they were in the other's house, while they were out in the mist playing hide and seek. It had been fun.

The tide was on the turn, and Thomas kept an eye on the horizon and the swelling haze. He knew the dangers of getting trapped by the tide on the Point. The wind was beginning to pick up, buffeting the mist which was churning towards the sandbank.

After another twenty minutes, he could hear the seals barking in the distance. It was the peak season for the pups. He loved that sound. He could sense their presence on the spit but couldn't see them. The mist cloaked the shore and was thickening with every minute.

He slowed his pace to avoid disturbing the creatures. He should have put on his wellies, he thought, as his shoes crunched on the shingle. He was starting to feel hungry and he didn't want to get home after his mother. He got into trouble when he did that.

As he turned, he saw a dark shape in the mist.

As it got closer he could make out the form of the dog racing towards him. It bounded forwards with its ears back and jaws gaping.

He looked round in panic. He couldn't see more than a few yards and felt completely alone. No one would hear his cries for help. There was nowhere to flee on the shingle. If he made a run towards home, he would be going straight towards the dog. The other way, towards the seals, led to a dead end on the spit.

Thomas decided to be brave like Eddie. He would make the dog turn back, like he'd seen Eddie do. He still had the stick, his Jedi sword.

He was mesmerised by the dog's burning eyes. The beast was as big as a horse. It made no sound. He raised his arm to command the dog to obey. He would not be afraid. He swirled his invisible cape around his shoulders and pointed the blade, saying, "Gaargh!"

The dog stopped. It sat on its hindquarters, watching, with its head on one side and its tongue lolling out of its mouth. Its ears were standing to attention.

Thomas stood his ground and waited. The beast got up and he dropped the stick. Thomas decided he needed to be tougher. He raised his arm again and held up two fingers, pointing as though to shoot an imaginary pistol, yelling, "Bang, bang!" But it didn't turn back like it had done with Eddie.

He crashed to the ground, crushed by the weight of the dog on his shoulders.

Chapter 30

Clayton led his team into the incident room. DCI Bligh stood in front of a desk with her legs crossed in front of her. She addressed them in the quiet voice she reserved for major setbacks. "We're going to have to tell the media about this. News will leak out anyway, after the boat chase." She looked around at their faces. "So where do we think this fugitive warden might be?"

"The dinghy turned up in Cromer. He'd tied it to the pier," said Clayton.

"Hmm," said Bligh. That was quite a way. The other side of Sheringham. It would have been dark when Jarvis reached Cromer.

"He could be anywhere now, of course, ma'am," Clayton added. From Cromer, he could take the train to Norwich. And from there, to London. "We're checking his card use and that kind of thing. Digging up background on him. And issuing an appeal. He's desperate, so we should warn people he may be dangerous. And we should probably contact Interpol as well, in case he tries to flee the country. He knows all the waterways."

"Right. Was the gun licensed?"

"Yes. It's legit, ma'am. It's a double-barrel twelve-bore. Perfect for shooting wildfowl, the wigeon and teal they get on the marsh. He left it in the boat."

"Wise move, probably," said Bligh.

"We're hoping for DNA clues from the car. Fifi, I mean Fiona, and her team are going through it now. And Jarvis' home in Branstable is being searched."

"Good. But it'll come as a shock to people that the suspect in this case is a nature reserve warden. What on earth was his motive?"

"That's the problem." It paid to be honest with Bligh.

"So what do we know about this guy? He lives in a caravan, right?"

One of the constables spoke up. "He's a bit of a drifter, actually ma'am. We can't find any relatives because he was adopted. He's never really lived anywhere permanent since he was a child."

Bligh adjusted her specs. "So where was he brought up?"

"Bristol," Julie said. "After school, he trained to be an electrician, then he moved around until he came to Glaveny, where he's been for the last six years."

"Right."

Clayton was urgently in need of a bacon sandwich. "Anyway, his behaviour is so suspicious that we'll have to name him as a suspect. And he lives within sight of the place where Emma Dawson's body was found. If he killed her, it would be quite possible for him to have kept her body in his car boot and dumped it in the boat in darkness."

"What about a connection to the dead boy in the churchyard?"

"We still don't know. Maybe we might get lucky if forensics come up with something on Jarvis. They're going over his car now."

"So does that rule out the French guy?"

"Not necessarily. I'll have a chat with the French detective to see where things stand. The only evidence against him so far has been circumstantial."

Neil interjected. "Jarvis was prepared to kill his colleague. We've got witnesses."

An officer came in from the direction of the control room. "We've had a 999 call from a woman in Pelham. Her child's gone missing."

"What's the name?" said Bligh.

"Sadler. Thomas Sadler. He's eight. He was supposed to be at home when she got back from work, but there was no sign of him."

"Oh God," Julie said. She flushed as everyone turned to look at her. She glanced across at Clayton. "The prophecy's come true!"

Chapter 31

Michel Billard was sweating.

He'd just finished twenty press-ups on the cold prison cell floor and was sitting on the bed eating a banana. Neither he nor his two cellmates looked up when the door opened and his lawyer entered. He noticed her violet fingernails clasped around a file. Her crisp presence had been his only contact with the outside world for the past two weeks.

"You're out," was all she said. "Come and get your things."

Billard stood up like a robot, his eyes wide in disbelief.

She said, "We've just heard from the Brits. They've another suspect in the murder case of Emma Dawson. We're going to see the judge now. She may decide to let you out on bail, given what we've just heard."

Billard couldn't speak. His legs began to shake.

The examining magistrate sat behind an ornate desk covered in paper files. She informed him that a certain Jean-Pierre Rossignol had agreed to stand bail.

"Jean-Pierre!" How could he ever make it up to his friend? And thank God they hadn't approached his parents.

"Yes, monsieur. But you must stay in France. To this end, we are confiscating your ID card and your passport."

They shook hands. Less than an hour later, after signing the release papers and recovering his things, he waited for a bus to take him back into St Valéry. But he had nowhere to go. He couldn't return to the apartment on the Quai du Romerel, and he doubted that his tent would still be at the campsite.

He walked up the Rue des Moulins, his backpack over one shoulder, and saw Rossignol's bike leaning against his wall. His friend came to the door and clapped his hands on his shoulders.

"Thank God! You're free. I'm so glad to see you."

"I can hardly take it in. I don't know what happened," said Billard, accepting the offer of a coffee and following him into the kitchen. Billard craved a cigarette but was determined to stop, to save money. "Thank you. They told me you'd paid the bail for me."

Rossignol waved his hand. "Forget it. How are you?"

"Never better. There were three of us in the cell, and we had to take it in turns to sleep on the mattress."

Rossignol exhaled and took another puff on his cigarette.

"There was a murderer in there with me!"

Rossignol flicked ash into a saucer. "Let's find out what's happening, and why they let you out."

He took out a laptop from a drawer. Billard told him to google the website of the *Eastern Daily Press*. He gasped when he saw the main headline.

It wasn't what he was looking for. "There's been another murder in Glaveny!" he said. "What the hell's going on in that place?"

He translated the headline for Rossignol. It read: 'Eight-year-old boy mauled to death on Glaveny Point.'

"That's where the seals are. Wait, what else is there?"

He scanned the other articles on the home page until he saw the headline he was looking for: 'Waitress' murder: warden sought.'

"This is incredible! I met this guy. Here's his name — Jarvis. Now they think he's the killer! That's ridiculous. These English cops, they're always after the wrong man!"

The paper had a box with the police number to call in case of a sighting of the fugitive warden.

Billard sat back, shaking his head. "Can you believe it?"

Rossignol stubbed out his cigarette. "What are you going to do now? Do you need to stay here? I can put you up while you find somewhere."

"I'm going back."

"Where?"

"Glaveny."

"How can you do that? They've got your papers! They'll arrest you again if they catch you." Rossignol put a hand on his shoulder as though to restrain him.

"That's why I want to go back. I didn't do anything wrong. I think I know the killer. Maybe I can help."

Rossignol stood up. "Help? How in the world can you help?"

"I'm telling you, they've got the wrong guy!"

Rossignol saw him clenching his fist. "What do you mean?"

"You know the waitress who was killed? She had a boyfriend. He's the murderer! He must have killed her when he found out about me and her."

"So she already had a boyfriend when you shagged her?"

"Yes, but I didn't know! She never said anything to me! Who else could it be?"

Rossignol shrugged. "Well, the Brits seem to think it's someone else. The warden."

Billard was still sitting at the computer. The caffeine had sharpened his thinking and he was already planning his journey. "Do you remember those migrants we saw, when you told me that you were a police informer?"

"I wouldn't call myself that exactly."

"Okay, but do you still see the boats come in?"

Rossignol turned down his mouth. "Not for a while, no. It's December. Must be too hard for them in the winter weather."

"Okay." In any case, it was too dangerous. Billard imagined a small craft weaving its way among the towering container ships in the shipping lanes. He stood up to go. If he wasn't going to go across in a migrant boat, following the currents to Norfolk like the seals, he'd have to find another way across the Channel. There was only one other way he knew, for someone without papers or money.

"Do you need some cash?"

"I'll pay you back."

His friend went to a drawer and took out some notes. "I knew you were innocent."

Billard looked at him hard. "What about the people at the seal association? What do they think? Will they have me back?"

"Don't worry. I'll have a word with them. And we'll help you get a job when you get back — if you get back."

"I'll be in touch. I'm going to get Emma's killer if it's the last thing I do."

Chapter 32

Bob Jarvis opened his wallet. He had £100 left.

He was the first customer at Morrisons when they opened the doors. He'd spent a cold night beside a pile of firewood at a petrol station, with only his fleece to keep him warm.

He made straight for the sandwich section and snatched an all-day breakfast triple pack from the fridge, with a bottle of water. Then he headed for the self-service checkout to pay. But something made him stop by the newspapers. He was all over the front page. They'd published a grainy picture of him from the nature reserve's website.

He thought quickly about what else he'd need to survive. He found the clothes aisle, grabbed a dark blue knitted hat and headed for the self-service checkout.

"Excuse me, sir."

Jarvis' heart thudded. He was almost out of the door.

"You dropped this," said the shop assistant.

He grabbed the hat and hurried out of the shop.

He pulled it on and zipped up his fleece against the wind as he walked past Cromer's red Victorian turrets in search of the warmth of a coffee bar to plot his next move.

He knew that by now his phone would be unusable and that the police would be onto his credit and debit cards.

He ordered a small filter coffee, and pretended to look at the cakes on display. He sat down in a corner of the café, facing the wall. Even this corner was brightly lit.

Hunched over his coffee, he weighed up whether to take the train to Norwich or to double back to Glaveny. The latter option might be smarter. Glaveny would be the one place the police wouldn't expect him to turn up in. And there were plenty of places he could think of to hole up for a few days until the media storm died down. On the other hand, there was always the possibility of a chance encounter with someone who might recognise him.

"Sir?" Jarvis jumped.

"Your change." He noticed the waitress' swollen red hands when she put down the coins on the table.

He pocketed the money and surreptitiously got out his sandwich. He shouldn't make a move before dark. They'd have found the boat by now, so the police would know he was in Cromer. He cursed himself for leaving the shotgun in the boat. But then he'd had no option.

He left and walked up the hill, past red-brick terraced houses. He realised as he reached Cromer station that the police station was on the other side of the road. What an idiot! He cast a sidelong glance at the squat brick building, and its half-empty car park, and quickened his pace. He kept going along Holt Road, past new housing developments and factories. He stopped for a while on a wooden bench outside a church graveyard.

A man with a corgi greeted him. He muttered a reply and pretended to look for something inside his bag.

He dropped his phone in a rubbish bin on the outskirts of town, rummaging through scraps of food for a newspaper. He was out of luck. Seeing a row of shops, he went inside a Boots where he bought some shaving things and a pair of socks. Did he have a Boots card? No. They're not going to trace me that way, he thought to himself. He could almost feel the CCTV drilling into the back of his neck as he pulled out some cash.

He made his way back to the town centre via a different route. He picked up some cheap underwear in a store on the seafront. Then he transferred all his belongings into one plastic bag.

In the afternoon, he ducked into the warmth of the Regal Cinema. He randomly picked the Paddington Bear film and bought some popcorn to stave off the hunger pangs. It was too early for a school audience and the multiplex was almost empty. Nobody paid any attention to the man in the woolly hat sitting in the back row. When he came out, the dark welcomed him.

The bus made its way along the coast road. The driver didn't even glance at him as he bought his ticket. Jarvis got off just before Pelham and walked towards the sea. If he saw any dog walkers he would get out of sight. He hiked through waist-high reeds, his eyes adjusting to the dark.

He saw the flashing police lights from a distance. The car seemed to be parked at the end of Beach Road. He wondered whether to retrace his steps but was drawn to the scene, where onlookers had gathered. He didn't see anyone he knew. He approached the small group slowly.

"Something happened?"

A grey-haired woman in a scarf answered without turning round. "Tommy Sadler. He's been killed. Mauled to death."

Someone else pointed towards the shingle spit and the seal colony. "Over there. They found his bike at the car park."

The little group huddled together, exchanging information.

Thomas Sadler! Another of the boys from the school, he thought. How could Mother Julian still be making her influence felt in this little community? The bitter taste of bile rose into his throat, and he began to feel nauseous.

"Oi!" someone called out. "Isn't that the guy they're looking for? The warden? His picture was in the paper. Oi, you!"

Jarvis felt the flash of a torchlight coming for him, and heard others call out to the police. He broke into a run and ducked into the sheltering marsh, protected by its whispering darkness.

Were they following him along the footpath? He didn't dare turn round. He stumbled on a stone, and slipped in the mud, falling to the ground with a curse. He turned to listen. Should he dive into the grass or keep going along the path? The shouting receded into the distance. He picked himself up and ran for his life.

Chapter 33

"Congratulations on being our splash for two days running," said the reporter from the *Eastern Daily Press*.

Clayton resisted the temptation to slam the phone down on the cheeky bastard. He had the paper right in front of him. He didn't need to be told what the headline was.

"What about the Black Shuck angle, Inspector? Hadn't there been sightings before the last kid died?"

"I already told you, Luke, I'm sorry, but you're not getting anything out of me today. You'll have to talk to our press office about this."

"Oh come on. Off the record."

"Gimme a break." He went downstairs to the cafeteria and picked up a bacon sandwich and a coffee. Other officers were beginning to filter in and he nodded to a couple of them. His phone buzzed just as he got back to his desk. He hoped it wasn't Bligh again. She'd already been onto him about the sighting of Jarvis on the marsh. At least that meant they could narrow the search area.

"There's a Mr Spratley in reception for you, sir."

Clayton struck his forehead with his hand. Why was this happening now? Maybe Julie could take care of the bereaved father.

"Give me a couple of minutes."

Jimmy Spratley's father was waiting in the lobby. He strode towards Clayton as the lift opened and looked as though he was deciding whether to shake him by the hand or grab him by the throat. The last thing he needed was a public scene.

"Mr Spratley, I wasn't expecting you. Come with me."

Clayton led him into a small interview room and offered a chair. Spratley remained standing. He had a prominent Adam's apple which bobbed up and down. "My wife and I are at our wits' end. We want to know what's going on in the investigation into Jimmy's death. The police have told us nothing and now we read in the newspaper that you think there's a connection between his murder and that waitress!"

"I'm sorry, Mr Spratley. The family liaison officer should be able to tell you."

"Well, she doesn't seem to know the slightest thing. Have you any idea what my family is going through?"

"I can tell you that we do believe there may be a link between the two murders, yes."

"But now you've got a new suspect? What happened about the Frenchman who was arrested? How can we sleep in our beds at night with a killer on the loose?"

"We have a strong suspicion, yes, that the runaway warden may be responsible. But until we catch him, there's no certainty."

Before Spratley had a chance to mention Thomas Sadler, Clayton added, "You may have seen that another boy from the school was killed on the marsh. We're not sure there's a link to the other two."

Spratley spat out his disgust. "So that makes three murders in Glaveny! If you ask me, you Norwich police need to do a better job of keeping people safe in our village."

Clayton moved towards the door. "Believe me, sir, we're doing our best. In the case of the investigation into Jimmy's death, we'll definitely keep you better informed in the future."

Spratley left, ignoring Clayton's outstretched hand.

Julie was at her work station googling 'causes of OCD.' She quickly shut down the screen when she noticed he'd seen what she was doing.

"Don't give me that look," she said.

"What look?"

"Like I'm to blame for Thomas' death."

"Weren't you supposed to get in touch with the schools about keeping their kids at home at night?"

"I did that, of course. I spoke to Thomas's headmistress personally. So it's not my fault if they didn't spread the word."

"I know. Sorry. I've just had Jimmy Spratley's dad in here shouting at me. We're going to have to find him a new FLO as they've lost all confidence in the last one. He's got a point. We've not been keeping them up to date with the investigation."

"And I suppose that's my fault too, is it?"

Clayton turned on his heel. "That's enough, Julie."

Neil was at the coffee machine. He pretended to be afraid when he saw the scowl on Clayton's face. "Having a bad hair day?"

Clayton touched his bald patch. "I always have a bad hair day."

Julie sidled up to them. "I've got a suspicion about the dog that savaged Thomas Sadler. The hermit has a vicious Great Dane, you know."

Neil turned to her. "That's weird, I've just been thinking about what I saw at his place."

"What do you mean?" said Clayton.

"He keeps a Great Dane in his back garden," Neil said. "A bloody big black thing."

"You mean it might be the dog that killed the lad?"

"You bet. Aren't Great Danes hunting dogs?" said Neil.

"I've seen it too," Julie said. She told them how she'd watched the dog hunting seagulls on the marsh. "It's quite fierce, actually. The hermit had a terrible time getting it back on the leash. I was scared it might come for me."

"You might be onto something there. Let's check it out, Neil. I need some fresh air anyway."

Chapter 34

It was raining by the time they got to Pelham-next-the-Marsh.

"The weather's so crappy he has to be in," Neil said. He knocked on the front door of the hermit's cottage. It opened a crack.

"What do you want? Did you catch those yobs yet? I think they've got my Caesar."

The two detectives looked at each other.

"Could you let us in?" Neil said. "We think you can help us."

The door opened and they went inside. Hopking took them into the dining room, where cat fur lay thick on the chairs.

Clayton introduced himself. "We're here about the murder of Thomas Sadler."

The hermit blinked. "It's got nothing to do with me."

"Mr Hopking, we believe it was your dog that chewed up the first boy's heart. And we also believe that it was responsible for the death of Thomas, your neighbour. Where do you think the animal is?"

"You tell me! Caesar means everything to me, you know. He'd never do anything like that. Those youths who come in from Wells or Holt must have snatched him. The ones I told you about," he said, looking pointedly at Neil.

"What's happened?"

"I found the gate open. He got out."

He gripped the edge of the table and sat down. "What are you going to do with him?"

"Right now, we're going to look for him. We presume he's wandering on the marsh. But when we find him, we'll have to get him put down I'm afraid, once we've got proof that your dog did kill Thomas."

"Put down?"

Neil glanced round the room. He breathed in the smell of rotting cabbage mingled with that of cat pee. A cat's eyes stared at them from under the table, unblinking. A black cat bounded onto a chair cushion and began licking its back leg with a rasping tongue, its ears pricked and its eyes on the visitors.

Hopking was shaking his head. "But why would Caesar kill a child?"

"Because the dog was starving. Famished," Neil said, more unkindly than he intended. "It ate the boy's face after mauling him."

He saw a tear glisten in the hermit's good eye. Hopking put up a yellowed hand to wipe it away. He wasn't looking at them anymore.

He sat back in the chair, and murmured to himself, "Come back, Caesar. You're my only friend."

Clayton and Neil left him to his thoughts, carefully navigating their way round the pet bowls and cat litter trays out of the house. Outside, the rain was pouring.

"I feel sorry for the poor guy," said Clayton, filling his lungs with fresh air. "Let's have a look round the back and see what's happened."

The wooden gate was hanging wide open. The heavy choke-chain lay useless on the ground beside it.

"Christ," Neil said. "How did they keep a dog that size under control, and take its chain off?"

He looked inside the makeshift wooden kennel, which contained nothing but a well-chewed piece of rug.

"Do you believe him? What if he let the dog out himself? We know he takes it out on the marsh."

"Could be. But why would he leave the leash behind? If it were youths there must have been several of them," said Clayton. "We'd better get some shooters out on the marsh, anyway."

"What? We can't just send marksmen out without warning people."

"You're right. I'll give the nod to the EDP. They were following up the Black Shuck angle on Thomas Sadler's death. This'll give them something to get their teeth into."

Neil grimaced. "*Police shoot Black Shuck*. I can just imagine the headline. Five hundred years of folklore gone in one shot."

"Never mind Black Shuck. A starving dog could kill again. And what about Jarvis? If he's desperate, so could he."

Chapter 35

Billard's lift dropped him by the roadside. He could see a group of people standing nearby. The dual carriageway curved round in a long arc towards the port. In the distance he saw long lines of traffic and parking areas lit up as bright as day. For the migrants in Calais the green lights on the ticket booths were the gateway to freedom.

He approached them cautiously, speaking in English. "You go to England?"

It was a man and a woman with two young children. They nodded.

"And where do you stay?"

"The Jungle."

"Can I go there with you?"

They were Africans and spoke to each other in a language he'd never heard before. They seemed to be hesitating. If they went back with him now, they might lose a chance of bundling into a lorry bound for Dover. The man shook his head.

"Food? In the Jungle?" Billard raised a hand to his lips and pretended to eat.

The man had understood. He pointed towards the gravelly path of a disused railway line.

"Where are you from?" he asked the man.

"Eritrea."

Billard wasn't exactly sure where that was. "Long way?"

"Yes. You know Djibouti? We are near."

Billard smiled. "Ah, okay, I see. Very long way." He waved goodbye and set off towards the path where he made his way carefully by torchlight, his feet catching in the undergrowth.

He'd read about conditions in the migrant camp they called the Jungle and he smelt it long before he saw it. Finally he reached his destination. He kept going along the muddy pathways past makeshift shelters until he reached a derelict warehouse. The stench from the piles of rubbish outside made him gag. They went inside and he gasped. The hall was filled with blue and khaki tents in all shapes and sizes. Sleeping bags were everywhere. It was home to hundreds of people, sheltering from the elements.

Billard joined a queue and was handed some sandwiches and a bottle of water. As he tore into the bread a heavily-built African man made his way over.

"England?" he said in English to Billard.

Billard nodded.

"You got eight hundred euros? Come tomorrow night."

"I don't have eight hundred."

"You a Frenchie?"

"Yes."

"Why don't you take Eurostar?"

Billard shrugged. "No papers. Long story."

The man moved on.

Billard looked at his watch. It was still only nine o'clock. Why waste another day waiting in Calais when he could try to get onto a lorry that night? The heat from all those bodies was making him sweat and he was glad to feel the cold slap of the wind on his face as he left the hall.

He was not alone on the old railway line. Many people were climbing out of the undergrowth in the shadows and crossing the road on their way to the lorry parks ringing the port. There was room to move four or five abreast. He wondered whether the family of Eritreans had already made it onto a truck. He watched as one group scrambled over the fence into a parking zone which was lit up brightly to deter the migrants. They must have paid the €800 to a people smuggler, he thought.

But no sooner had they landed on the other side when security officers ran out from behind a lorry, firing pepper spray. Some had dogs. People began running in all directions. He could see some migrants bent double, while others shouted out to each other in distress.

Now's my chance, he thought, hurling his backpack over and taking a running jump at the wire fence. He managed to propel himself over. He was aware of others coming out of the bushes to try their luck. He landed with a crunch and remained on the ground while he made sure he was okay. He grabbed his rucksack and crept round the lorry park, examining the back doors of each vehicle carefully before picking his target.

The first truck was so firmly locked it would have taken a minor explosion to blow open the door. Billard's mouth was dry with fear as he went along the line of parked lorries, trying one after the other, all the time listening out for the sound of police or security guards. Halfway down a second line of lorries he felt a door yield to his push. Opening the door by a crack, he was confronted by a wall of cardboard boxes. He saw a space along one side and clambered in, pulling the door shut behind him.

He heard something rustle. "Who's there?"

A torch shone in his face, blinding him.

"Police?"

It was a question, not an announcement. The relief made him giddy.

"I go to England," he whispered.

The torch lit up chiselled features.

"From Afghanistan," the young man said. "We go together."

He held out his hand and helped Billard squeeze himself next to him at the back of the lorry, as far inside as they could go. It was stifling. Billard had to stand with his stomach pulled in and his hands at his sides. They didn't dare speak. Time passed, and the lorry did not move. He began to wonder whether their journey would even take place that night. How long could he stand it in here without suffocating?

Then the doors were flung open and torchlight played over the cardboard boxes. Was it the driver or the police? Billard heard coughing outside. Did they have dogs? He held his breath, grateful for a whiff of fresh air but praying that the doors would close again.

The doors closed and the truck lurched into life. They were on the move.

Chapter 36

"No sign of the missing warden, I suppose?"

Bligh rarely made an unannounced visit to Clayton's desk. She was wearing her coat. This must be serious, he thought.

"He was spotted where Thomas Sadler was killed, then he disappeared into thin air. But we presume he must still be in the Glaveny area. Before that, the search was concentrated on Cromer, where we found his phone. And he was caught on CCTV outside the cinema there."

"So the suspect returns to the scene of the crime?"

"Well, no one's suggesting Jarvis had anything to do with Thomas' death, ma'am. In fact, we could have sent dogs out to help catch him, but that would be a bit tricky, what with a manhunt *and* a dog hunt going on in the marsh. A recipe for chaos."

She nodded. "You got a minute?"

"Sure," he said.

"Right, let's go out," she said. It *was* serious.

Clayton picked up his jacket and followed her to the lift.

"Where to, boss? I'll drive."

"The Mad Hatters?"

It was a tea shop in Wymondham about a five-minute drive away. In the old days, Clayton thought, they would have gone to the pub for a pint.

As they exited the car park, he told Bligh that Neil had teased him because he didn't know it was pronounced 'windum.'

"A few of the names round here took me some getting used to as well, when I came from Brixton. Like Pelham. All the locals say it *Plum*," she said.

"I only found that out after Jimmy Spratley was murdered," Clayton said.

They sat at a table by the window and ordered two teas. Would it be too much to ask for a scone as well? Don't push your luck, Clayton decided.

"Shall I be mother?" she said.

He put some milk into his tea cup and noticed that she poured the tea into hers first.

"Mother Julian?" he said.

"Actually, this isn't about the case. That's why I wanted a private word. I'm going to have to take one of your team," said Bligh.

It was the moment he'd feared. "I was half-expecting that, ma'am, I must say."

Bligh shrugged. "But who's it to be? That's my dilemma."

Clayton put two teaspoons of sugar into his tea and stirred vigorously.

"I'm inclined to pick Julie over Neil," said Bligh. "She's from Suffolk and she joined us after Neil. It would probably cause less of a fuss with the Police Federation."

She raised a finger to her lips. She wore no rings. "This is between us, of course. Julie's a woman and I can't be seen to be discriminating in any way. I can't let her family situation influence my recommendation either, although I know she's bringing up a child pretty much on her own. But then Neil is the breadwinner in his family, and he's got two young kids. So, on purely professional grounds, I just wondered what you'd say."

"It's a tough one," said Clayton. "I wouldn't want to lose either of them. It has to be one or the other?"

Bligh nodded. "I need the savings. I've looked at every permutation I can think of. Sorry."

Clayton said that Julie was motivated. She had taken a particular interest in the Glaveny murders, maybe because of her young boy. She was proactive, and had volunteered to take round the witness appeal, which was a thankless task that someone else could have done.

"On the other hand, she's got a tendency to go freelance," he said.

"What do you mean? Not moonlighting? Or is she a loose cannon?"

"Loose cannon? Oh, God no. She just needs to refer things upwards, keep everyone in the loop, and not just follow her own hunches. Not a big deal." He realised he'd already said too much.

"And what about as a work colleague?"

Clayton scratched behind his ear. "As you've probably noticed, she's had a sense of humour bypass. And then there are the tensions between her and Neil."

"That's not a capital offence. What we want are results. What about him?"

"He's a good cop. Smart. Possibly a bit rigid. Can be an arrogant bastard too."

"Promotion material?"

"I'd say Julie, of the two of them. But Neil is desperate for a promotion. Not to mention his two ex-wives would probably be overjoyed. I'm glad it's not me who has to choose."

Bligh stared into her tea as though it were a crystal ball. She lowered her voice. The café was starting to fill up with customers taking a break from Christmas shopping. "So you've got some shooters out on the marsh now, looking for that dog?"

"Yes. And I just got off the phone with the warden, Mike Skipper, who's keeping an eye out too."

"Good. We can't afford another death, for Christ's sake. And this disappearing warden worries me. If anyone knows the marsh, he does."

"Yes, ma'am."

Bligh stood up and fastened her coat. "Right, well, you know how important this case is. If it falls apart, I don't think we'd just be looking at Julie and Neil." She gave Clayton a meaningful look.

She paid and they offered their seats to a couple coming in from the cold with their packages.

But Clayton felt cornered. Why did it have to be his team? Couldn't they find other candidates for redundancy? He could think of plenty of dead wood.

* * *

Neil was waiting for him when he got back. "Great news!"

It would have to be a major breakthrough to improve Clayton's mood.

"The techies have found a DNA match with the girl in the warden's car!"

"Bloody fucking fantastic!"

"He's a size nine too. They also found a DNA trace from Jimmy Spratley, the boy in the churchyard. That means that the two killings were definitely linked! It looks like Jarvis is a double murderer."

He held up his hand to receive a high five, but Clayton ignored it.

"So now all we have to do is find the bugger. Just imagine if we had a serial killer on our hands."

Chapter 37

Billard's breath froze in the air as he walked slowly down the lane towards Branstable Quay. He noticed crime-scene tape around a caravan in the caravan park. Was this where Jarvis lived? Looking down the lane towards the sea, he could make out the welcoming light of the nature reserve visitor centre.

When he reached the car park, he saw more tape around the boat where Emma Dawson's body had been found. He felt the anger rising inside him. How could they have suspected him?

He'd survived the hot and airless lorry journey to Dover, and the uncertainty every time the vehicle came to a standstill. He and the Afghan had parted company at a petrol station in Kent. Parched and sweaty, they'd banged on the door so loudly that the driver had come running and opened up. He'd screamed at them that he'd lose his job but they pushed past him. Customers filling up their tanks had stood and laughed in surprise when the doors were flung open, watching them flee.

He pushed open the door to the visitor centre. Mike Skipper was at the counter, writing something in a book.

The warden looked up. "Holy shit!"

Billard grinned.

"What the hell are you doing here? Last thing I heard, you were up for murder."

Speaking slowly and quietly, Billard said, "It wasn't me. I've come back to help find Emma's killer. I see they're looking for your colleague, Mr Jarvis."

"Well, I'm not sure how the police would react to *your* help," said Skipper.

"Is that his place? The caravan?"

Skipper nodded. "The one up the road? Yes. Where are you staying while you're here?"

"I thought I'd try a bed and breakfast again."

"At this time of year?"

"I'm afraid there's another thing. I've not got much money."

Skipper offered to help him find a place to stay and made a couple of calls. He managed to secure a room in a house off Glaveny High Street belonging to a friend. He got out a map and pointed it out.

"How will you get there?"

"On foot."

"Okay, but stay away from the marsh. They've got shooters out there looking for a killer dog on the loose. It'll take you a good half hour to walk along the main road from here."

"Don't worry. I know the way, I'll be fine, thanks," said Billard. He took down Skipper's phone number, picked up his backpack and headed off.

As soon as he got to the main road, he held up his thumb and hitched a lift to Oak Farm. He ignored the barking dogs as he walked up the drive and made his way to the outhouse in search of his rival. It was empty. He went straight to the barns. Hay was piled high inside. Mellor was nowhere to be seen.

The walk back to Glaveny along narrow lanes took him almost an hour. He knocked on the door at the address Skipper had given him. It was a small flint cottage tucked in an alleyway and reminded him of Emma's place. A Christmas tree stood in the corner downstairs. The young couple were friendly, showed him to a small room upstairs and gave him a key.

"This is very nice," he said. "I'm very grateful. I only need a night or two."

"No worries," said the woman, noticing him fumbling for his wallet. "Mike's a good friend."

He took a quick shower and headed out, leaving his backpack behind but taking his torch to help find his way along the unlit streets.

He walked to the Harbour Inn. He'd never seen it so crowded, the noise was deafening. He stood by the door while he adjusted to all the people speaking English at the top of their voices.

He made his way to one side of the pub. A group of men was playing darts. One of them was Mellor. Billard hesitated. Should he get a drink? He looked at the bar and saw that the redheaded barmaid wasn't there. That might be lucky for him. He didn't want to draw attention to himself. All he wanted to do was deal with Mellor and get the hell out.

He stood beside the farmhand just as he was about to throw, and whispered in his ear, "Come outside." Mellor was so surprised that the dart fell from his fingers and into the wooden floor with a thud, missing his foot by a couple of inches.

"Who's this?" said one of Mellor's mates. "Shall we get rid of him for you?" They began to move towards Billard, pushing him roughly to one side.

"I can handle it," said Mellor.

Billard had forgotten that Mellor was bigger and more powerful than him, but he seized the initiative, caught the farmhand by the arm and steered him towards the door. They were back in the pub garden where they'd had their last confrontation.

"I'm here to take revenge for Emma," Billard growled. "I've got a knife. I know you killed her!"

"What are you on? Why would I kill her? The police thought it was you!"

"You killed her because you were jealous. A crime of passion," Billard said. "It's obvious!" He didn't care who could hear him shouting.

"It wasn't me, I swear," said Mellor. "They're after the warden. He came to our séances at Emma's cottage."

"Séances?" These Brits never ceased to amaze him. Billard got out his Laguiole knife and flicked it open, holding it under Mellor's chin, his hand trembling slightly. "How do I know you're telling the truth?"

"Cos I am." Mellor raised a hand and forced Billard to lower the knife.

"I just want to find the one who killed her," Billard said. Had he come all this way for this?

Mellor twisted away and began walking back to the pub. "Now piss off home, and leave me alone, you French twat."

Billard sat down at a bench table outside and put his head in his hands. He couldn't afford to stay much longer for what was turning into a wild goose chase. He was hungry. Maybe he'd be able to get something to eat on the High Street on the way back to his lodgings.

He set off again. The moonlight was bright enough for him to make out the colours on the Glaveny signpost on the little village green. As he walked along the quay, he noticed a pinprick of light out on the marsh. The light was about 100 metres away, on the other side of the car park. It was coming from inside the cabin of a rusted old boat. It was keeled over on one side, obviously dumped on the marsh by a tidal surge. As he strained to look, the light went out. Was he imagining things?

He stood still for a second and gazed at the sky, where the stars glittered like a jewel box. It reminded him of home. Up there was the Great Belt, and over there, the

Plough. He found the pointer star in the saucepan of the Plough and followed it towards the North Star.

As his gaze descended, he saw a wisp of white drifting over the marsh in the moonlight. Was it a cloud? Or mist? He waited until the sky cleared again. He loved these clear, crisp nights. He resumed his stargazing in the stillness of the marsh. Then he saw the swaying light again, inside the boat, just for a moment.

His instinct was to flee. It wouldn't take him more than a couple of minutes to run back to the safety of his room, but he felt weighted down in his boots. Then he decided to investigate. This was why he'd returned to Glaveny after all. He looked round. There was nobody in sight. He curved his hand around the Laguiole in his pocket.

What if it was the murderer? What would he do? He got out his phone and rang Skipper.

"Michel Billard here. I've seen a light in a boat near the Point Hotel. I thought it might be something."

"Are you sure?"

"Yes. Well, no. It was there but now it's not."

"Well, don't move and don't do anything. I'll call the police and get someone down there right now," said Skipper. "I'm coming over too."

Billard waited in the cold for a couple of minutes. He wondered how long it would take for the police to arrive. Then he crossed the car park to get closer to the boat, which lay across a mud channel. At that moment, the light reappeared but went out again after a few seconds. His blood went cold.

Slowly, he advanced, trying not to make a sound. His hiking boots scraped on a narrow wooden bridge over the waterway. The muddy banks gleamed in the moonlight.

He realised he was panting. He'd almost reached the boat when he heard a rasping snarl behind him. A giant dog was coming towards him from the darkness of the channel. It came slowly out of the creek, ears pricked and fangs bared. He'd never seen such a huge dog. It shook itself, sending flying the mud caked on its powerful body.

The effort seemed to force it back onto its hind legs, and it sat for a few seconds. Then it raised itself again to its full height and lunged at him, its jaws wide open.

Chapter 38

"Jesus Christ, Sam, it's amateur hour," Bligh said.

"Well, at least we got the bloody dog." Sam Clayton saw her look at the stuffed seal and felt embarrassed. "I'm sorry. The first thing I knew about the Frenchman being back here was when the warden alerted me after they found him on the marsh. That thing had mauled him to within an inch of his life."

It was lucky, thought Clayton, that the Wells police officer who rushed to the scene had had the presence of mind to call in one of the shooters, who'd finished off the Great Dane. The dog was howling and writhing in pain after Billard had stabbed it.

"So where is he now?"

"Norwich hospital. Intensive care."

Bligh crossed her arms. "At least he's alive. Can you imagine the fuss if we had another dead body in Glaveny? And what about the fugitive warden?"

"He escaped. We're pretty sure he'd been hiding in the boat, but he must have heard the kerfuffle outside. He was in such a hurry he left the door open. There were empty sandwich cartons inside."

"And what about the car? We're sure about the DNA match with the girl?"

"Absolutely, ma'am. Jarvis had cleaned it out, but we found a hair which matched Emma Dawson's. So it looks like he killed her, kept the body in the car, and then heaved her into the boat when all was quiet."

He paused. "Then there's the dead child. His DNA was also in the boot. Now we know for sure that Jarvis murdered them both, but we don't know why." He made a mental note to ask Julie to brief the new FLO for the Spratley family.

Bligh sighed. "Okay, I'll have a word with the press officer about this. The way to present it is that we're closing on the suspected killer and we've put down the dog that killed Thomas Sadler."

"Jarvis will be desperate by now, particularly if he's living on egg sandwiches. He can't have got far, so we can step up our patrols."

Bligh stopped looming over his desk. Clayton picked up his phone. He wondered what Claire would say. Billard was being treated at the hospital where she worked.

She answered straight away. "It's chaos round here."

"I can imagine. Sorry. Didn't see it coming, I'm afraid." Why was he apologising to everyone? None of this was his fault.

"Well, we've had reporters crawling all over the place to get a look at Our Hero the Frenchman. One even dressed up in scrubs to get into his room!"

"Hero?"

"Well, they're saying he killed Black Shuck, the devil hound that mauled poor Thomas Sadler, that's what. The amazing thing is that he's the same guy you suspected of being the waitress' murderer!"

Oh, what was the point? Clayton dreaded to think what the French authorities would say about Billard popping up in Glaveny. He'd better call Gallois.

"There's going to be a press conference later. Let me know if you need help in keeping the hacks outside," was all he said.

Claire had always been able to see through him. "Hey! How are you anyway?"

"Bit stressed. I'll feel better when we catch this bastard."

"Keep in touch," she said, and hung up.

The seal was looking up at him with its head cocked to one side. Clayton picked it up and chucked it into the wastepaper basket.

* * *

The weekend was approaching. The searchers had found nothing on the marsh, and Clayton began to worry about newspaper headlines accusing the police of letting Jarvis get away.

It was a grey Saturday afternoon. Clayton forced himself to spend a couple of hours practising scales and *apoyando* exercises, but his heart wasn't in it. He couldn't stop thinking about the manhunt on the marsh. Where could Jarvis be hiding? What if he'd gone back to Cromer? Surely if he'd tried to rent a room in a local hotel or bed and breakfast, someone would have come forward? Or he could be somewhere like Oak Farm, in one of the outhouses, sleeping on the hay bales. But the police had visited all the farms around Glaveny and come back empty-handed.

They'd also questioned ticket sellers at the railway station and the bus station in Norwich. Every line of inquiry had been a dead end.

By five o'clock, he could stand it no longer. He'd been over and over the case so often that he was even starting to doubt that Jarvis was the killer. He went out to the car and drove to the Harbour Inn in Glaveny.

He recognised Len Maitland the painter, who was sitting on a stool drawn up at the bar, his bad leg hanging by his side. He doffed his cap at Clayton. Was that sarcasm by any chance?

Clayton sidled over to the barmaid and asked her about Jarvis. She didn't answer immediately.

"I don't know if he has any real friends here, to be honest," she said eventually. "Was that Adnams you wanted?"

He nodded and she poured him a pint. "Make that burger and chips too," he added.

Her earrings glowed in the light. "He gives me the creeps, actually," she said. "He kept himself to himself pretty much."

"He didn't keep to himself that much. Don't forget he was a member of your club. And what do you mean, he gives you the creeps?"

She shrugged. "Nothing. Just saying."

"So you can't think of anyone he was close to here who might give him shelter?"

"Not really. There are the farms I suppose. He could doss in a stable, couldn't he?"

"Of course. Our guys are onto it." He wondered why he'd bothered to drive to Glaveny. He went to a table where he finished his pint in silence and wolfed down his meal. He noticed that the pub was half empty.

He went back to the bar. "Where is everyone on a Saturday night?"

Jen shot him a look. "Think about it. Everyone's too terrified to go out."

Clayton was aware that Maitland had leaned towards them, listening. He jiggled the coins in his pocket, lost for words. "We're doing our best," he said eventually. He took a couple of steps towards the door, hesitating. Should he say something more reassuring? He turned round. "Well, goodnight."

* * *

He drove to Branstable Quay. He got out of the VW and looked towards the horizon, where dark clouds were about to envelop the spit. He zipped up the anorak over his jacket and noticed a solitary boatman securing a boat in the wind.

He looked out across the creek, thinking. Of course! Jarvis would have a key to the wardens' place. It was closed for the winter and he could have bolted there after being discovered in the abandoned boat.

He approached the boatman. "A storm coming?"

"Can't you feel it?" As he spoke, the first drops of rain began pattering onto the ground.

"I'm police, Anglian Constabulary. CID. I need to get to the Lifeboat House in a hurry and the quickest way is by boat."

The boatman looked dubious but began to untie his little motor boat.

"Hold onto your stomach!" Even in the creek the wind was whipping up the waves. Holding onto the side, Clayton called the office and asked the duty officer to find out when the searchers had last checked the Lifeboat House. It had been three days since they had.

Zipping his phone into a pocket, he pulled up his hood and faced into the wind behind the boatman. The rain was lashing down, piercing the water. The drops streaming down their faces were icy. As they reached the open waters and headed towards the Lifeboat House on the southern shore of Glaveny Point, Clayton began to feel queasy. Burger's revenge. The boat crashed into the waves, bringing him almost to his feet with every lurch. They reached the shore, and the boatman splashed into the water in his wellies, holding the rope. Clayton realised he wasn't properly equipped. The water came up to his knees and he gasped from the cold.

But they were in luck. He could see the glow of a lamp inside the building's dark hulk. Then it disappeared. Jarvis wasn't taking any chances.

"You stay here," said Clayton. "I'm calling for help." His fingers white from cold, he texted Bligh and Neil and began squelching towards the building. The path was slippery with mud.

He went round to the side, marched up the steps and rattled the door. "Jarvis! I know you're in there. Open up. Police." He sounded more courageous than he felt. There was no sound inside. "Police!" he yelled again, and banged on the door. "Open up or I'll break the door down!"

Clayton was almost stuttering with cold. With a huge effort, he put his full weight behind the door. It flew open on the second push, projecting him into the room where he struggled to keep his balance.

He knew he was vulnerable. He blinked in the darkness. He guessed that the warden was accustomed to the shadows and had the advantage. Clayton knew he mustn't let Jarvis rush him and escape into the marsh again.

"Jarvis! Come out. You can't escape. We've got you covered."

Where was he? Clayton could make out a table and chairs but nothing more. A moment later, a figure emerged from the darkness and grabbed his legs. Clayton fell onto the floor, winded. The pain was excruciating. He forced himself to sit up, and grabbed the foot just about to deliver a kick. He twisted it with all his strength and heard the sound of a body crashing to the wooden floor. One all.

Then Jarvis was on top of him. He was heavy. They fell back down, both panting from the effort. They rolled from side to side, arms thrashing. They were both the same height, but Jarvis was more muscular. His hands dug into Clayton's flesh, while Clayton's were so cold they couldn't get a proper grip on the warden's jacket.

Clayton felt Jarvis trying to reach for something inside his jacket, and worried that he might have a knife. But that split second gave the detective time to stand up unsteadily and reach for a chair.

As he turned away, Jarvis gave him a hard push from behind. It sent him flying into the table. Clayton hit it with a thump and Jarvis made for the door.

Chapter 39

Bligh had just put the kettle on when her phone buzzed with Clayton's text message. Another Saturday night gone. Not that she had any plans.

She made herself a cup of tea anyway and called Neil. "You'll have seen Clayton's message? He's gone boating. Terrible weather for it."

"Yes. I called Wells and they're sending someone over."

"Good. Fine."

"Should I go down there myself?" he asked. "Should I let Julie know?"

"No. They're closer. Let's leave it to them." She rang off. Then she thought again. If it all went pear-shaped, she'd be responsible for the decision to leave backup to the local police. She set down her tea on the kitchen table, took off her glasses and rubbed her eyes. She took her mug upstairs and drew the curtains in her study. On her desk were photographs of her parents, and the nieces and nephews whose Christmas presents sat in a corner of the room, ready wrapped. All signed, 'with love, Aunt Charlotte.'

She'd never married. Most of her colleagues were single but scarred by at least one divorce. The closest she'd come to tying the knot had been in her twenties. But he'd been another cop, and the thought of spending her entire life at work was more than she could bear. Now, twenty years later, she was doing just that. She remembered the training course where they'd got together, the way they'd concealed their relationship from colleagues for the first few months. And then they'd had the embarrassment of a very public split. She grimaced at the memory.

She switched on the desk light and opened her laptop. She'd never had a case like this, where the seemingly supernatural collided with real life. It was as though everything was covered in mist, and there were no clear lines of separation. Even if Jarvis had committed the murders, was he just a tool?

She drummed her fingernails on the desk. They had to be missing something. The answers must lie in Emma Dawson's file. Maybe there was a clue in her profile that they'd overlooked. Was she really just a medium? Her parents said she had changed after she met that cult leader. Was she channelling Mother Julian for her own purposes, grooming her victims by 'testing' them first?

Bligh looked up from her work. Could Emma Dawson really have been so sinister? Perhaps she too was controlled by forces from the past. "Ridiculous," she said out loud, and snapped shut her laptop.

* * *

Julie was enjoying a carefree Saturday night. She watched her son trying to wind tinsel round their Christmas tree and winding it round himself instead. He was screaming with laughter.

"Ollie, I thought you were supposed to be helping!" she said.

"Give us a twirl," said Paul, who was on his knees picking up the baubles that kept falling off the tree. "Hey, look at the time. It's past your bedtime. Get on with it."

The decorations done, the three of them stepped back to admire their work. The blue lights blinked like a police siren. Julie took Ollie upstairs for his bath and heard Paul switch on the television downstairs. She heard a phone ringing in the bedroom. It must be his, she thought, and went to answer. "Paul's phone."

It was a woman's voice. "Hello? Oh I'm sorry, I've got the wrong number."

Julie looked at the number. The caller was identified as 'Meredith.' She dropped the phone onto the bedside cabinet as if it were on fire, and went back to the bathroom to dry Ollie off. She packed him into bed.

"No story tonight, sweetie." Julie wanted to throw up. She was remembering all the times in the last few weeks that she'd called Paul when he should have been at home and it had gone straight to voicemail.

"Why?" Ollie's eyes creased and his face puckered.

How clever they are when they want something, she thought. Just like his dad. "No. Not tonight." She got up, but turned back at the door. "By the way, how's Eddie doing?"

"Oh alright. Yeah, alright."

"Is he talking now?"

"Yes. Good night." Ollie turned his back to her. She planted a kiss on one cheek before going slowly downstairs.

She sat next to Paul on the sofa and picked up a yellow cushion, holding it to her. In a low voice, she said, "You've just had a call from your friend Meredith."

"Oh yes?" His feet stayed stretched out in front of him, and he put an arm behind his head. "What did she want?" He was staring at the television.

"Well, she said it was a wrong number. Which it obviously wasn't," Julie said, bringing her face close to his.

He drew back ever so slightly. "What's going on? Tell me the truth!"

He pressed the mute button on the remote and folded his arms. After a long pause, he looked at her and whispered, "Nothing's going on. She's a friend from the station, that's all. A DC."

Julie's arms hung limply by her side. She should never have left Ipswich. She'd trusted him too much. "Well, if you don't feel like telling me, you won't mind sleeping on the sofa tonight, will you?"

She put on the TV sound again and went to check on Ollie. As she reached the bottom of the stairs, she turned to say, "For a detective, you're pretty crap at covering your tracks."

Chapter 40

Jarvis stood at the threshold of the Lifeboat House for a few seconds, his chest heaving. He emerged, blinking, into the rain.

The punch floored him.

The boatman had arrived like an avenging angel dressed in shiny yellow. Detective and warden picked themselves up slowly, while the boatman guarded the entrance. Jarvis was cornered.

Breathing with difficulty, Clayton seized him by the arm and said, "Bob Jarvis, I arrest you on suspicion of the murder of Emma Dawson."

Jarvis didn't struggle. In fact, he appeared to be relieved.

Clayton escorted him back to the boat. The boatman waded into the water, apparently oblivious to the cold, and clambered aboard first before helping them in. They sat in silence on the way back to the quay, Clayton touching a swollen lip and clutching his chest. His limbs had stiffened in the cold. Jarvis was crumpled in a corner.

They could make out the flashing blue light of a police car on the quayside. A constable was standing in a dinghy moored at the quay.

"What took you so long?" Clayton said.

The officer checked his watch. "Less than half an hour since they called us, sir. Have you noticed the weather? And we had a car crash as well. Couple of louts from the estate slid off the road." The young officer studied the detective and his prisoner. "You okay? Did you know you've got an open cut on your head?"

It was only then that Clayton realised it wasn't rain running down his face. When he looked at Jarvis, he thought the boatman had probably broken his nose.

"Nothing like a bit of mud wrestling on a Saturday night."

He was about to climb into the car, when he stopped. "What was that you said about louts?"

"Yes, sir. Saturday nights. It's always the same ones, they seem to enjoy racing between Branstable and Pelham. It's a long straight line. But this time one of their cars came a cropper outside Glaveny."

"Anyone hurt?"

"Not seriously. The other car carried on to Pelham. A red Fiesta. They're probably still in the Victoria there now. We couldn't even charge them with speeding as there were no witnesses."

"No speed cameras?"

"No, sir. Not on that stretch."

"Interesting." He walked a few paces away, took out his phone and called Neil.

* * *

The two youths stepped out of the pub just before closing time. Neil heard their coarse laughter as they walked towards the Fiesta, which blinked when the remote unlocked the doors.

Neil had jumped into his car, high on adrenalin, as soon as Clayton had called. "Sorry, pet, bit of an emergency," he'd said to Megan. "I'll make it up to you."

"You always say that. I don't know why you bother." He'd left her watching TV with a glass of wine beside her.

He wondered whether he should go straight to the address that Clayton had given him in Wells but decided to head for Pelham. It was easy enough to find the car outside the Victoria, its doors spattered with mud. He took out his torch and looked inside. A sports bag lay on the back seat.

He got back into his car, switched on the radio and waited. The Victoria, a timber-framed building with an annex facing towards the sea, was busy. A group of young people, the girls wearing strappy tops and high heels, smoked on the steps. How come they never get cold, he wondered, as an image of his teenage daughter came into his mind. She was sixteen now, and lived with his first wife, who'd moved to Leicester. He'd seen her go out bare-legged in midwinter, waving away his "silly old fart" protests.

He watched the pair get into the Fiesta, and heard the noise of the engine revving. Then the warning lights came on. It was still stationary.

"Shit," Neil said under his breath. What was going on?

Then a flimsily-clad girl came running out of the pub and got into the back seat. They must have been waiting for her. The youth in the front passenger seat joined her and they began snogging.

The warning lights went off and the Fiesta turned left out of the car park without indicating. Neil followed at a discreet distance. It sped away until it reached the hermit's cottage, then slowed almost to a standstill. He couldn't be sure but the passengers seemed to be talking animatedly. The house itself was in darkness.

They're showing off to the girl, he thought.

On the other side of Pelham, the car in front accelerated again. Neil let it pull ahead as it was doing 70 mph on the main road, whose speed limit was 60. As he'd expected, it slowed down on the other side of Glaveny. He saw them pointing excitedly at the silver Nissan overturned in the ditch. They carried straight on to Wells, in another burst of speed.

A few minutes later, Neil followed them down a drive of pebbledash houses. With surprise on his side, he jumped out of the car and rushed to the driver's side as the door opened, holding up his warrant card.

"Police!" he shouted. The back door on the opposite side shot open and the two occupants ran off down the street, hand in hand. Neil paid them no attention. He could smell alcohol on the breath of the driver, a youth with ear piercings and a buzz cut.

"Underage drink driving, are we? Get out of there, you varmint. You're nicked." He grabbed hold of the youth. He could tell from the captive bicep that its owner had spent hours in the gym.

"I'm eighteen. You can't touch me."

"We'll see about that. This your car?"

The boy struggled. "My dad's."

"He in?"

"Dunno."

Neil glanced behind him and saw no lights on in the house, whose front path led past a low stone wall. He checked the papers in the glovebox and dragged him back to his car to breathalyse him. He sensed the youth was no longer quite so confident.

"So your dad's Roger Stonehouse. And what's your name?"

"John."

"Right, Johnny." Keeping hold of the boy's arm he opened the boot, took out the breathalyser and waited. "Hmm, twice over the limit. Your goose is cooked, Johnny, and it'll be even worse for you and your friends if you don't cooperate." Neil tightened his grip on Johnny's arm.

"What's the matter, Johnny? You don't mind harming poor animals but you don't like someone hurting you."

The youth looked startled. Neil pressed his advantage. "We're onto you. You're bullies who've been harassing a harmless old man. It was you and your gang of lowlifes who stoned the hermit's Great Dane in Pelham. We know you let it out. And do you know what it did then?"

He noticed the youth looking round for a means of escape, and tightened his grip. "It mauled an eight-year-old boy to death! That's your fault!"

Johnny started to tremble. "We didn't know it would do that!"

"Lock your car. We'll just go inside so we can see how old you are really, and then you're coming with me to the station," Neil said.

* * *

Two days later, DCI Bligh was standing with Julie and Neil behind the one-way mirror of the interview room.

Jarvis and Clayton limped towards the table in the centre of the room. Jarvis' lawyer trailed behind. "They make a pretty pair," said Bligh. Jarvis' nose was bandaged, and Clayton had stitches over one eyebrow.

Clayton switched on the recorder and read the warden his rights once again. "Let's have a look at your tattoo then."

Jarvis checked with his lawyer before rolling up a trouser leg. The daisy motif was just above his ankle.

"Have you ever done drugs, Mr Jarvis?"

He looked startled by the question.

"Coke? Other recreational drugs?"

He shook his head.

"That's a no, then."

Jarvis looked at the tape recorder. "I've never taken drugs."

"So, now, let's hear all about it. The Glaveny cabal. When did you first get involved with Emma Dawson and her crew?"

Jarvis leaned forward and the story began to emerge. "I went to a séance for the first time about a year ago, not long after Emma came to Glaveny. I was impressed by her psychic powers."

"Such as?"

"She was obviously in touch with Mother Julian."

"Obviously?"

"Yes. Her behaviour was completely different, her voice and everything. As time went on, the core group became closer and we all had tattoos done to show our membership."

"So if you weren't under the influence of drugs, how did she persuade a guy like you to get a tattoo?"

"I'm telling you, she was powerful. It was incredible to think we were actually in touch with Mother Julian. Looking back, I think we must have been hypnotised, although we didn't realise it at the time. That only became clearer later, when Mother Julian began testing us."

"Testing you? How?"

"Emma'd say that Mother Julian wanted a sacrifice, and one of us would have to get rid of a dog or a cat. I only know that because that's what the others told me. For me it was much worse. Emma said to me, 'Mother Julian wants a child.'" He sat back staring into space, as though reliving the moment.

Behind the glass, Julie looked at Neil. "Christ! So that's what Eddie must have heard. He knew Jarvis had killed Jimmy Spratley, and that's what he drew later in those pictures we saw."

Bligh put a finger to her lips and their gaze returned to the room. Jarvis was now gripping the table as though to keep steady.

"Then what?" Clayton said softly.

"I was on the marsh one evening, not too far from Emma's place. There was nobody around, and I saw this boy on his own: Jimmy Spratley. I knew him from a school group. I . . . I don't know what came over me." Jarvis swallowed hard. "You'll never believe this, but I really didn't realise what I was doing when I stabbed him. My car was nearby, and I took him to the churchyard, where someone else had already dug a grave. It was only when I found myself wandering on the marsh in the dark with his heart in my pocket that I realised what I'd done."

"Why didn't you come forward then?"

"I've been asking myself that ever since. But I didn't. I couldn't. None of us could. We'd all been sworn to secrecy. Then I thought that the only way it would all go away would be if I got rid of Emma. She was the cause of everything."

"Was it a chance encounter?"

"Yes. I didn't plan anything. How would I know I'd see her? It was a misty afternoon and I ran into her on the marsh near the windmill. I doubled back to a fence, stripped off some barbed wire and went back to her again." His eyes begged them to believe him.

Clayton remembered something. "Was that the day you told Skipper that you had a migraine?"

Jarvis looked surprised. "Yes, it was."

"And that night you took her body to Branstable Quay in the car."

The warden glanced at his solicitor, then nodded.

"And what about the knife?"

"I took it back to the caravan and washed it. Then I realised I couldn't keep it and buried it in the field over the fence from the caravan park."

Clayton closed his notebook and stood up. Then, as though remembering something, he sat down again. "There's one thing I still don't get."

Jarvis sat, feeling his bandaged nose, waiting for the question.

"Why did you really keep going back?"

Jarvis hesitated, shifting on his chair. His eyes darted sideways to his solicitor. Then he said, "My parents."

Chapter 41

Behind the screen, Julie tensed. For a moment she felt sorry for the warden. She glanced at Bligh and saw that she was staring fixedly at Clayton. Julie worried that Clayton might ruin everything with his impatience. Go gently, she thought.

Clayton leaned back in his chair, arms folded. "Okay, what about your parents? You lost them, right?"

Jarvis kept fiddling with his bandage, beads of sweat forming on his forehead.

"That's right. They both died in a car crash when I was very young. I was raised by foster parents. But I never knew what happened to my real parents and I thought I'd find out something about them at the séances with Emma."

"Ah. And did you?"

Jarvis took a hanky from his jeans pocket and mopped his forehead. "Once, yes. It was quite incredible. I could swear Emma was in touch with my mother, Christine, on the other side. There was a swirling in the room, like smoke or vapour going upwards, and we had a sense that there was some kind of presence with us. I definitely felt it. Whatever it was, the swirling was right around me."

"And?"

Julie saw the tell-tale signs of Clayton's mounting impatience. His foot was tapping on the floor.

"Well, that's what made me think Emma had really contacted her. But just as she was getting going, the candle went out and that was it."

"What do you mean?"

Jarvis looked flustered and took out the hanky again. "She said the spirit had gone. But she promised to try to get in touch again after we did what Mother Julian wanted."

"But she never did."

Jarvis said nothing.

Julie was thinking about how much she missed Caroline. But would she ever have contacted a medium? You poor, manipulated fool, she thought, staring at Jarvis.

* * *

They had to push through a scrum of journalists waiting outside the nick. Clayton overheard a group of them speaking French. He caught sight of Luke Martin from the EDP and gave him a thumbs-up. When the reporter indicated that he'd call him, Clayton shook his head. The boss was handling this. She basked in the glory while Clayton only got to explain the failures. Bligh had even come in this morning with a new haircut, cropped shorter than usual.

Clayton, Neil and Julie piled into a police car. "Drink driving?" Neil said.

"Just a quick one," said Clayton. "They built this place in the middle of nowhere for a reason, you know!"

They parked outside the Smugglers Inn in Wymondham and went into the snug, where a fake fire was doing its best to pretend it was alive. Clayton bought a round and they stood and gave each other high fives.

Clayton raised his glass. "Here's to us, team!"

"So are you okay?" Julie said, tapping her eyebrow.

He smiled. "It's the two broken ribs that hurt. Comes with the territory, though."

"So your rugby playing days are over," Neil said. "I must say I was surprised by how Jarvis cracked and coughed up the whole lot in one go."

"It's often the way. He wasn't a hardened criminal. He just got caught up in something he couldn't control. He seemed almost grateful to be caught," said Clayton.

"So what happens now?" Julie said.

"Well, you'd better make sure that the Spratley family is properly briefed, for one. We don't want him having another tantrum in reception," said Clayton. Julie nodded.

"And then we go back to our day jobs," Clayton added.

"If we still have them," Neil said.

They laughed, but it sounded forced.

Neil turned to Julie. "How come you got so interested in child protection?"

She flushed.

"Sorry, I didn't mean to . . ." For once, Neil seemed genuinely apologetic.

"No, that's okay." She took a deep breath. "I had a daughter before my son was born. She died."

"I'm sorry," said Clayton. He looked away in case she began to cry.

"It was a cot death. She was only eighteen months old . . ." her voice was beginning to crack, but she carried on. "The worst thing was the post-mortem. They had to make sure it wasn't child abuse. Can you imagine?" She looked at them with an embarrassed half-smile. "But anyway, that's the long answer to your question."

Clayton and Neil stared into their pints.

"Look, I didn't mean to put a damper on things," she said. "We're supposed to be celebrating. Merry Christmas!" She raised her glass and they clinked.

"Your little Oliver though," said Clayton. "He's six, right? Same age as Eddie Dawson?"

She could see what he was driving at. "That's right. He hasn't got the same dad as Caroline. My current partner stayed behind in Ipswich when I moved here with Ollie."

"So you split then?" Neil asked.

"Actually, no. Not technically, anyway. Not then. But jobs and marriage don't go together like a horse and carriage."

They all smiled.

"Wow, that's a lot to take in all in one go," said Clayton. What would have happened if he'd left Claire behind in Lancashire, he wondered. He was pretty sure she'd never have visited him in Norwich. What a modern marriage that would have been.

"So absence doesn't necessarily make the heart grow fonder? Anyway, moving on, you've done a great job with the kids on this case."

"But there's one thing I still don't get," Neil said. "Why did Jarvis get mixed up with that lot in the first place?"

"I think he must have got a sense of belonging from joining the group," Julie said. "And from what he said just now, it sounded like Emma had some kind of hold over him because of her contact with his parents. Frankly, after losing Caroline, I can understand that. Or maybe that's what he was searching for all the time. A new family."

Neil snorted. "Come to Glaveny for a slice of village life, complete with crazies and poltergeists!"

Clayton ignored him. "I think Julie's right. Maybe he just wanted to belong. Look at his background."

Neil raised his glass for a clink. "And then Mother Julian comes along, and he's got a new mummy!"

Julie pulled a face. "You really are incorrigible." She gave a weary smile, and touched glasses.

"Anyone want crisps?" said Clayton.

When they returned to the office. Clayton contemplated the piles of papers on his desk as though it was the first time he'd noticed them. He resisted the temptation to sweep them onto the floor. He sat at his computer, singing the melody of the *Concierto de Aranjuez* to himself.

"Di di dee. Dah di dee dee dee dah di di dee." I'm free, he thought. What would he do with his weekends now? He'd have all the time in the world to sell the house and find a nice little two-up two-down. Maybe a fixer-upper. With a smaller garden. Definitely. But first of all, he'd take a holiday. Go home in the new year, back to the fells. The trouble with this place is it's too damned flat, he thought. Claire was right.

His phone rang, interrupting his reverie. It was Bligh.

"Can you come up?"

Chapter 42

"I've discovered something about Emma Dawson which I think has been overlooked," said Bligh.

Was he about to get a bollocking? Clayton sat down and waited.

"You must be as curious as I am about the actual motive for these murders. Well, I think I found a clue in an interview which Julie conducted with Emma Dawson's parents. They said she'd been hospitalised after having a breakdown, and had been given pills. But I can't find any reference to what kind of diagnosis she was given, what sort of pills and whether she was still taking them."

"Leave it with me."

"Do you see what I mean though?"

"I do, yes." Clayton felt like kicking himself. This was embarrassing. He walked slowly down the stairs and made for Julie's work station. It was piled high with books on the occult.

"The boss thinks that Emma Dawson was a psycho."

"What? That's ridiculous. Psychic perhaps, but . . ." She turned round in her chair to face him.

"She's just given me chapter and verse on the interview you did with her parents. They told you she'd had a breakdown and was on pills."

"Yes. And?"

"What sort of breakdown? And what sort of pills? Don't you see, Julie? We dropped the sodding ball."

"There's no need to fly off the handle with me," she said. "They were bereaved. They'd just lost their daughter. I'm sorry but I must have felt that I couldn't press them about it."

"Well, maybe you could now. Give them a ring and let me know what they say."

He went back to his desk and turned to look at the map on the wall, on which each pin marked a tragedy for a family in a North Norfolk village. The three deaths had traumatised an entire community. What more could they have done to prevent them? He saw the empty wastepaper basket standing by the window. He stretched out his leg and sent it flying.

A few minutes later Julie came over with her notebook, her lips pursed.

"I've spoken to Mrs Onslow. She said that as Emma wasn't living at home at the time, they only found out about her breakdown after she was out of hospital. They never knew what she was put on, either." She raised her chin defiantly.

"Okay. Which hospital?"

"Norwich."

"Thanks."

It's a start, he thought, picking up the phone. He wondered where Claire would be at this time in the afternoon.

She answered immediately.

"Can you talk?"

"Just let me shut the door."

He heard the phone being put down, then a door clicked. He tried to picture her at her desk. "This is urgent.

I need a favour. You know this Glaveny murder case? Well, it turns out that the waitress who seemed to have been pulling the strings before she was murdered had actually been at your hospital for a spell."

"What, recently?"

"No. It was a few years ago, before we arrived. But I need you to help me find out what she was diagnosed with."

Claire put on her prim voice. "I can't give you medical records, you know that."

"I don't need them, we can get a court order to get the records from the GP. But I just need to know what she was in for, to save time. Without getting you into trouble, obviously."

"What was this woman's name?"

"Emma Dawson. Actually, Emma Onslow. That was her maiden name. I was thinking that lover-boy might be able to help. He was in neuropsychiatry, wasn't he?"

"You mean Simon? Yes, he is." Clayton was surprised he'd remembered this. "But if you're expecting me to approach him with a request like that, you've got another thing coming!"

He knew he'd gone too far. Claire hung up without saying goodbye.

Chapter 43

Clayton passed by the tray of sizzling bacon and went straight to the coffee bar. He stopped to chat with a couple of officers, picked up the sugar, then brought the drinks over to Julie and Neil. They'd found a quiet corner of the cafeteria and taken out their notebooks.

Clayton put down the cups. "What have we got then?"

"I checked the evidence files and there was no sign of any pills at the house," Julie said. "So presumably she wasn't on medication at the time of her death."

"Okay. Well, I've just heard from a little bird that she was hospitalised with a delusional disorder and was on antipsychotic drugs. Neuroleptics." Clayton couldn't resist a triumphant swig of his coffee. He put the cup down loudly onto the saucer and licked foam from his lips.

"Wow!" Neil said. "That all makes sense."

"Yes. She was off the meds! She was off the fucking meds!" Clayton spoke so loudly that heads turned in their direction.

"What exactly is delusional disorder — apart from having delusions?" Julie asked.

"My understanding is that there are several types. We'll have to make a formal request to get her medical records, but it looks like what she had is the grandiose variety, where patients get an over-inflated sense of their own power and their own self-worth."

"So you mean she wanted to impress them with her so-called connection to Mother Julian?"

"Right. If she really did connect. I think her *contacting the dead* was all a load of crap."

Julie looked uncomfortable. "She still had the power to put them into a trance though."

"Apparently she did, aye."

"She must have thought she was cured, otherwise she wouldn't have stopped taking the pills," Neil said. "Poor thing, those drugs are like a chemical cosh, aren't they?"

"Anyway, I'm going up to tell Bligh now. Hopefully that'll be the end of it. See you upstairs."

Clayton tidied his hair in the lift mirror and tapped the handrail as he waited for the doors to open.

Bligh's door was ajar, and she beckoned him in while she finished a phone call.

Without naming names, Clayton told her everything he'd got from Claire, who'd eventually relented. Bligh's eyes widened when he told her that Emma Dawson had stopped taking the antipsychotics after moving to Glaveny.

"I see. This puts things in a whole different light. You'll put in a request for the medical records?"

"Of course." He got up to go, but she called him back.

"There's something else, Sam." Something told him this wasn't going to be good news.

"I've done my list."

"The redundancies?"

"Yes."

Chapter 44

Julie's footsteps echoed as she made her way to a back pew at St Nicholas church. She watched the vicar of Glaveny finish off a conversation with an elderly woman who was arranging a Nativity scene in front of the pulpit.

Eventually he noticed her. "I was wondering how long it would take you to come back, Detective."

"Really? I've had a bit of a setback, actually," she said. "And that's rather an understatement. I've just lost my bloody job." As she said the words she could feel tears forming, and struggled to blink them away. She felt such a fool, driving all this way on an impulse to confide in someone. But who else could she talk to? Paul wasn't answering his phone, and she had no close friends on the force in Norwich. She could hardly pour out her troubles to Neil.

"I thought that you and your team were the heroes of Glaveny after solving all those murders."

"I'd have thought so too," she said, smiling wanly. "But that's not the way it works in the real world." She took out a tissue and dabbed her eyes. "Sorry."

"What will he get? The warden?" he asked.

"Life, if he's charged with murder. But he might plead diminished responsibility."

He stroked his beard, pulling the strands tight.

"And what about Emma Dawson? Fancy her pretending it was Mother Julian. It was a *perversion* of everything she stood for." He snorted. "That Emma Dawson obviously wasn't what she seemed."

"People rarely are, in my experience," Julie said. "Emma was obviously sick, disturbed, we know that now. But I think she was drunk on her power over others. It gave her a status she didn't have in the rest of her life."

He nodded. "Sometimes I think that the dead are like a cipher. People fill them with their own thoughts and feelings. I've seen it time and time again before a funeral when talking with relatives. The deceased take their secrets with them. And the rest is a matter of opinion."

A bit like my job then, Julie thought. She looked at her watch and picked up her bag. It was getting late. She had to get back to the nick.

"So tell me," the vicar said, "what are you going to do now?"

She sighed and felt her eyes cloud with tears. "I haven't a clue. It depends where I can get a job. God, it's such a nightmare."

"You mean you're not going to challenge the decision?"

"My partner wants me to move back to Ipswich with our son. But to tell you the truth, things aren't going so well with him either. Honestly, at this point I really don't know what I want. It might be a bit late now anyway to fight it, don't you think?" She turned to face him.

The vicar reached out and patted her hand. "Have faith in yourself. Go now and do something about it."

They parted. Julie walked slowly down the path in the dark, through the graveyard. She took out her car keys when she reached the row of parking outside the primary school. But then she hesitated. She kept going along the main road until she came to the cul-de-sac where Emma Dawson had lived. I'll just have one last look, she thought. This was where it had all started.

It was pitch black. A light was on downstairs in Becky Berry's house. A couple of cars were parked on the cobbles. Julie switched on the flashlight on her phone as she picked her way along the street. She stood outside the waitress' cottage and resisted the temptation to knock. She was about to walk away when a movement in the upstairs window caught her attention, and her heart almost stopped. Condensation was forming an odd shape with a watery swirl. She switched off the light and stared, blinking, at the vapour on the window. Am I seeing things, Julie wondered. She flicked the light back on and flashed it upwards. There was nothing there but condensation dripping down. She shook her head, and slowly followed the arc of the flashlight back to the main road.

* * *

Clayton was pacing around the house, thinking about Julie. He'd tried to fight her corner with Bligh but she'd said the decision was final.

Had he protected Julie sufficiently? He grimaced. Based on what he now knew, he should have kept his mouth shut. He regretted mentioning her "freelancing." That was unfair. And anyone would lose their sense of humour if they'd lost a child. When Bligh told him that Julie was to be made redundant, he'd pleaded with her to find another victim, saying that she'd had some hard knocks. It seemed unreasonable to target her, given the success of the Glaveny investigation.

The only outside chance was that Bligh hadn't yet sent on the list to the super. Might she have a Plan B? But what if the alternative was Neil? That would be just as big a disaster.

He opened the fridge door. The evening's supper was sitting inside, a choice between curry and lasagne. There were grease stains on the kitchen table. He took out a bottle of beer and kicked the fridge door shut. He heard the phone ring in the living room. It was Julie.

"Talk of the devil. I was just thinking about you."

"Really?" she said. "I just wanted to let you know that I'm going to fight this redundancy. I don't know yet whether to go to the Police Federation or just have it out with Bligh, but I'm not going to take it lying down."

"Way to go, Julie. If I were you I'd ask for a meeting with Bligh first. You don't want to piss them off by going crying to the union. You never know, she might be open to persuasion. I'm on your side, and I told her so."

"The witch didn't even have the courage to tell me herself. She left the dirty work to you!"

Clayton said nothing. He was glad she was ready to fight. She'd run from the office in tears.

"Right. I'll go see Bligh tomorrow, and I'll let you know what happens." She rang off.

Chapter 45

The DCI stood up to shake hands with Julie and motioned for her to sit down.

"I've come about my job," began Julie.

"I dare say you have," she said. "But regrettably . . ."

"Regrettably there's nothing to be done? Is that what you were going to say?"

Bligh seemed taken aback. Julie pulled back a bit. "I'd be grateful if you'd just hear me out. This job is hugely important to me." Please God, she said to herself, don't let me cry now.

Bligh opened her hands to indicate that Julie had the floor.

Julie leaned forward. "I'd like to talk about this investigation which we successfully concluded. I think that my role in the team was absolutely critical to the outcome."

A raised eyebrow.

"I was the first one to suspect a link between the murders of the boy in the churchyard and the waitress. I was the first one to take the paranormal stuff seriously. I was the one who ensured that the pictures of Eddie, the waitress' son, were taken seriously. In fact they actually *depicted* Jimmy Spratley's murder. And finally, I was the one who had the idea of a séance with Eddie, during which he identified Bob Jarvis as his mother's killer."

She sat back, unused to blowing her own trumpet. She hoped she hadn't forgotten anything.

Bligh looked as though she was hearing this for the first time. "Did you say 'séance?'" Bligh stood up and leaned over the desk. "With a grieving child? Had you completely lost your senses? This is the first I've heard about this!"

"I mean, it's what led to Jarvis' confession!" Julie flushed and began waving her hands around. "Actually it wasn't a séance. More a conversation with the boy. We got him to talk. Anyway, I got permission. His father agreed, and I checked with the boy's psychologist."

Bligh sat down again. "I see. But you didn't get permission from me, the senior investigating officer. DS Everett, if ever this should get out to the press . . . I mean, Jesus Christ!"

"It won't. I promise." Julie wished she'd never asked for the appointment. She wanted the chair to disappear through the floor and take her with it. Maybe going back to Ipswich with Ollie wasn't such a bad idea after all.

Bligh was as flushed as she was. The brunette and the blonde stared at each other in silence. Eventually Bligh said, "Leave it with me. I'll have to have a word with DI Clayton."

That sounded ominous. As soon as Julie was out of the room, Bligh sat down again, and checked the TV guide on her computer. She'd need to unwind tonight.

* * *

"So what made you go to see Bligh?" Neil said. "I'm impressed."

He and Julie were in the corridor outside the DCI's office by the coffee machine, waiting for the door to open.

Clayton had been closeted inside for the last half hour, and they could hear raised voices.

"You mean you didn't think I had it in me?"

"Touchy."

"Let's just say I realised that I couldn't just walk away from the job I love."

As she spoke, the door swung open and Bligh strode out. She didn't seem to notice the two detective sergeants. Clayton followed her out.

He waited until Bligh was out of sight, then said, "You might as well both hear this. Bligh's saved Julie's job and you're okay too, Neil. Congratulations!" Clayton heaved a big sigh. "Christ, that was touch and go."

"So who's for the chop?"

"Don't know and don't care. Just so long as our team's intact. Bligh promised me that she had another plan in mind. I always suspected she might have, but I couldn't be sure. Maybe she can find some voluntary redundancies."

Julie felt her legs begin to tremble. "Thanks, boss. Much appreciated."

"Anytime. Now let's get back to work."

Sam clapped Neil on the shoulder and they went downstairs to the CID suite. He settled in front of his computer, stroking the wound over his eyebrow, and turned his head to watch them go back to their desks. They were laughing. Clayton felt as though a heavy weight had lifted.

He glanced down at his phone and went through the contacts until he reached Claire's number.

As the phone began to ring he thought to himself, this is a mistake.

THE END

Acknowledgements

I would like to thank the following for their valuable contributions and insights as *The Marsh* progressed. They are: Mike Beach, Roger Browning, Geoff Carter, Margaret Crompton, Claire David, Mary Friel, Mike Gray, Heather Hill, Charles Kaye, Alan Newman, and my father Ted Penketh.

Any mistakes, of course, are mine alone.

Thank you for reading this book. If you enjoyed it please leave feedback on Amazon, and if there is anything we missed or you have a question about then please get in touch. The author and publishing team appreciate your feedback and time reading this book.

Our email is office@joffebooks.com

www.joffebooks.com

We hate typos but sometimes they slip through.
Please send any errors you find to:
corrections@joffebooks.com

We'll get them fixed ASAP. We're very grateful to eagle-eyed readers who take the time to contact us.

Printed in Great Britain
by Amazon

71209928R00139